THE WORST OF LUCK

BRITTANY P. JOSEPH

THE WORST OF LUCK

CONTENT WARNING

This book contains content/themes that may not be suitable for all readers, including: death, murder & attempted murder, graphic violence, rape, family trauma, emotional abuse, kidnapping, and abandonment. Please read at your own discretion.

CHAPTER 1

Being twenty years old has its advantages. Some include being out of school, gaining independence, and being able to do adult things.

Then there are the disadvantages: working as many hours as possible to make ends meet and still dealing with your parents. Those disadvantages sum up my life right now.

I tighten my ponytail that holds my light brown straightened hair and take a deep breath as I grab a wet rag. I head to a booth that I cleared of dirty dishes and started to wipe it down. Working as a waitress at a diner in Bay City, I work as many hours as possible to keep the house running. My mom, on the other hand, sits at home and drinks alcohol non-stop. She relies on me to pay the bills and keep the house clean. I even work on my days off to make enough money to put into my savings and pay the bills. I am determined to save enough to get my own place someday. I once saved up to buy my car a while back. If I can save for that, I can save for a place to live.

"Elizabeth, why aren't you cleaning table five?!" said Tammy Kartner, one of my co-waitresses. She gave me an angry look while holding one hand on her hip and her other hand was playing with her dark blonde and curly hair.

Tammy, the self-proclaimed queen of the diner, has worked here longer than most of us. Her belief in her superiority is evident in her excessive makeup and constant reminders of her seniority. Despite being in her late 30s, she still acts like a teenager, a fact that she takes pride in.

"Because that's your table and not mine," I said, trying to show her I was strong enough to stand up to her. I tried my hardest not to look nervous, as I always do around Tammy.

"It doesn't matter if it's mine or yours. You still need to clean it! I'm pretty sure Barbara and I agree that you're not fit for this job—well, pretty much any job in this world," Tammy started laughing. "I remember Barbara saying she wanted to see you in her office. You better pack up your apron as you head to her office."

Working with Tammy for as long as I have been at the diner has been challenging, mainly because of how she acts. She always makes me handle her tables along with mine and keeps the tips from her tables all to herself as if she did all the work. I've been wanting to speak to our manager about how Tammy has been treating me lately, but I never had the courage to do so.

I walked up to our manager's office and knocked on her door.

"Come in," Barbara said.

Barbara Girlfur is an amiable and calm manager until she has to be firm with someone. She's been managing the diner for a few years and is always on top of things. Being in her mid-fifties, she has a few wrinkles around her face, but she doesn't care about them because she always says, 'They are a sign of someone working hard throughout their lifetime.' She has thick blondish-red hair. She always wears a necklace with pearls on it, along with pearl earrings. Barbara always shows that age and wrinkles don't matter when it comes to great work managing the diner.

I opened the door and saw Barbara sitting at her desk in her small office. On her desk was a computer screen and mouse, a gold nameplate with her name on it, a coffee mug, and a cup with pens. On her wall were her college degrees and pictures of her family.

"You wanted to see me?" I said.

"Yes. Have a seat," Barbara said.

I started to get shaky as I sat in one of two seats in front of her desk. Was Tammy right? Am I going to get fired? I got increasingly nervous as I waited for what felt like a century for her to tell me what she wanted to see me for. I was even forgetting to breathe at one point.

"We have a new waitress starting tomorrow, and I want you to train her. She will follow you and watch what you do as you explain responsibilities to her," Barbara said. Hearing that was such a relief.

"Well, that's a relief. I thought you were going to fire me," I said.

"Why would I fire you, Elizabeth?"

"Because Tammy said you and she agree I'm not fit for this job."

"Oh really? Has she said anything else to you?"

"She was yelling at me for not cleaning her tables."

"I'll talk with her. Don't listen to what she says. You are nowhere near getting fired."

"Thank you, Barbara."

I couldn't stop smiling as I walked out of Barbara's office, mainly because I was not getting fired but also because Tammy was likely about to get a taste of her own medicine. If lucky, I would get to overhear that.

Tammy was sitting at one of my tables with her arms crossed. As I approached the table, Tammy stood up.

"It's nice to see you back, troublemaker. It's okay if you need to cry," Tammy said.

Barbara walked up behind Tammy as Tammy started laughing. "I wouldn't say that, Tammy," she said.

"What? Isn't she in trouble?" Tammy said as she turned around to face Barbara.

"No. You're in trouble."

"Why?"

"Because somebody said you were yelling at Elizabeth for not cleaning your table."

"I was only yelling at her because she wasn't listening."

"You know, we've been getting complaints about your behavior."

"Well, those complainers need to get used to it."

"Well, in that case, you're fired!"

"What?! You can't fire me! I've been busting my butt here for ten years, and I'm pretty much the only one here who knows what to do!"

"You mean by making others do your job?"

Tammy didn't know how to answer that. She quickly moved her head back and forth while trying to find a good answer, but she was unsuccessful.

"Now get out of my diner!" Barbara said.

Tammy walked out of the diner while looking toward the ground.

After Tammy was gone, I felt like I had lost a hundred pounds. I felt less pressure and could do my job without any issues. It was a wonderful feeling.

Although I had more work to do because the diner was short one waiter, I was glad Tammy wasn't constantly yelling at me. Plus, doing more work would mean time would go quicker. And with that, I would get rest before I knew it.

Even though I was thinking about the end of the work day, I never looked forward to going home for any reason other than to get some rest. My mom is not the loving and nurturing Mom everybody wants. Aside from her drinking alcohol from morning to night, she tends to be verbally abusive towards me. She always has been that way ever since I was a child. Thanks to that, my childhood was pretty much rough.

I have witnessed my mom get beaten up by my dad while growing up. Whenever I was home from school, I would hear yelling, big thud sounds, glass breaking, and doors slamming. I would hide in my bedroom whenever I sat foot in my house until I needed to get something to eat or go to the bathroom. My bedroom was always my safe place. It was the place I knew I wouldn't be involved in my parents' fights.

My dad lived with me and my mom until I was eight. One morning, my dad went to work and never came home. During one of Dad's breaks at work, he called Mom and said he would never return. Mom was devastated. She cried continuously throughout the night and hardly slept until she had enough alcohol to get her to sleep. I never understood why Mom was devastated by this because of how he treated her. I saw it as an opportunity for her to stop drinking and maybe have a happier life.

Mom kept trying to contact him and find ways to work it out. However, Dad responded to those attempts with divorce papers. They had been married for ten years. I have no idea how she survived ten years with him.

The divorce settled with Mom keeping the house they both owned. Mom also got full custody of me. How did she get granted full custody of me with her alcoholic needs? By playing the victim. She claimed that if she didn't drink the alcohol that he gave her, he would somehow physically assault her. She also claimed that she hadn't had a drink since he left because she didn't care about alcohol. Mom even went twenty-four hours without a drink to make it even more convincing and not make it evident that she still drinks. How did she survive that? She slept that whole twenty-four hours so she wouldn't feel a withdrawal. She saved a bottle of vodka for the celebration after the divorce got settled and went her way.

Dad, on the other hand, had to pay child support to Mom for ten years. And shockingly, he made every payment to her on time. When mom received those child support checks, she would pay bills with it. However, for the most part, she would buy any alcohol she could get her hands on. She relied on food stamps to put food on the table and has never held a job ever since I was born.

After I turned eighteen, Mom relied on me to pay bills and put food on the table. While I handled that, she applied for unemployment benefits. When she received her unemployment checks, she would spend it all mostly on alcohol.

I pull into the driveway in my red, beaten-up yet still drive-able Dodge Neon. As I parked the car I hesitated about walking into my home. On the outside, I see the pretty light blue small house I've lived in my entire life. It shows off like a happy family home with green grass, a couple of trees, and a fence around the yard. On the inside, it's a dark place—literally.

After sitting for a few minutes, wishing I didn't have to go inside, I exited my car and headed to the front door.

"Mom, I'm home," I said as I entered the not-so-lit living room through the front door. The blinds and curtains were closed, and the lights were off. The only thing on in the house was the television.

"Where were you?!" Mom said while taking a sip of her beer. Her dark brown hair looked like she had just gotten out of bed and was still wearing her pajamas from the night before.

"At work."

"Don't lie to me!"

"Why do you always assume I'm lying to you?"

"Because I'm your mother, and I can."

"That's not nice, you know."

"I don't see what's wrong with it."

I rolled my eyes. "Clearly."

I went straight to my room after that. I've had enough of dealing with Mom for one night. My bedroom is the happiest place in this house. Whenever I have a problem with Mom or want some alone time, it's the place to be.

My bedroom is small but big enough to hold a full-size bed and a little brown table. My only things are my cell phone, clothes, printer paper, pencils, and other necessities. My money gets spent on the bills and necessities for everyday living in this household and put into savings to get a place of my own someday—hopefully soon.

On a typical night after work, I play games on my phone or write/draw on paper. The most common thing I write on paper are my feelings, which I write like a poem. Sometimes, I draw or write stories, but writing my feelings out is what I do more often—tonight seemed like a night I just wanted to lay on my bed and gather my thoughts.

I put on my white nightgown (the only pair of pajamas I have) and then got myself in bed under the covers. As I lay on my bed and stared at the ceiling, I wondered how to move out and be on my own sooner. I've been wanting to move out since I was eighteen. Of course, I hadn't had any luck with that because buying my car didn't help with my savings, for starters. Knowing her and her reactions to things, I was also scared of how Mom would react. In my head, I kept trying to figure out ideas on how I could build my savings faster enough to move out sooner. Doing overtime at the diner was not helpful enough. I can't make enough soon enough. I continued trying to come up with ideas until I finally dozed off.

CHAPTER 2

I woke up to a bright and shiny day. I felt ready for a new day. Then I remembered that I had to face Mom before work.

"Where are you going?!" Mom yelled after I told her I was leaving.

"To work," I responded, trying to be calm.

"What?! There's no such way a girl as stupid as you could have a job."

"Well, I do. So goodbye."

I then walked out the front door and shut the door behind me.

It's not unusual for Mom to call me names and say things like I'm worthless. It does hurt to hear her say that, but I've gotten used to it enough to ignore it. Along with my ways of coping in my room, I also try positive thinking or listening to music in my car when I'm not in my room.

Once I arrived at work, I noticed Tammy was inside wearing her apron as if she were working. I immediately walked up to her after I clocked in.

"Tammy, what are you doing here? You got fired, remember?" I said. I smirked while waiting for her to respond, realizing I could confront her confidently. Beforehand, I would never have seen myself confront her like I just did. I would typically have left her alone and tried to finish my work while she yelled at me. It sure felt good to confront her for once.

"They decided they made a mistake and told me to come back in today," Tammy said as she put her hands on her hips.

"I call that a lie."

"Just get to work!"

I didn't believe Tammy one bit that she got re-hired. Knowing Barbara, I doubt she would bring Tammy back.

After dealing with Tammy, I met the new waitress. Jenny Harbor was her name, and she was around my age. While introducing ourselves, I noticed how Jenny kept ensuring all her straight brown hair was tied back into her ponytail. She also made sure no hair was on her face. I figured it was because Jenny was nervous about today being her first day. Other than that, she seemed nice. She was easy to talk to and seemed like a fun person to be with.

Jenny followed me around while I explained the responsibilities of the waitress to her, and my best friend, Martha Killsie, walked into the restaurant. Wearing her black shorts and white sparkly T-shirt, she adjusted her short, black curly hair while waving in my direction.

"Hey, Elizabeth!" Martha said.

"Hey, Martha!" I said, waving back at her.

Martha and I met in elementary school when we were ten years old. We always understood each other. Whenever I felt I had to get away from Mom, Martha always had a spare bed for me to sleep there. Her mom was like a nurturing mom to me.

Her mom made me feel like I had a mom I could go to for anything my mom couldn't offer. Martha and I always have fun together.

I told Jenny to take a break while I took mine with Martha. I grabbed sodas for Martha and me and sat down with her.

"How is life treating you?" Martha said after sipping her soda.

"Same as usual," I said.

"I'm sorry to hear that. Have you considered moving out?"

"You have no idea how bad I want to move out of there. But it's hard with my mom being the mom she is. It's also hard for me to save up enough to move."

Tammy walked up to our table in the middle of our conversation.

"Elizabeth! What are you doing?! Get back to work!" she said.

"Can't you see I'm taking a break, Tammy?" I responded.

"Where we work, there is no such thing as a break!"

"Why don't you just leave us alone?" Martha said.

"Oh look, it's loser number two."

"Excuse me?"

"You heard me, loser."

"Elizabeth, take her down!" By that, Martha meant to wrestle her to the ground. Martha and I promised each other, when we were kids, that whenever somebody hurt us emotionally or physically, we would stick up for each other by wrestling that person down to the ground. Of course, I didn't take that literally. I've always believed it meant to scare the person away.

"Tammy, leave us alone!" I said.

"Elizabeth, I said take her down," Martha said.

"Do you not see me trying?"

"No. I see someone not keeping a promise."

"What are you talking about?"

"Why are you not wrestling her to the ground?"

"I'm trying to figure out what to say to her."

Martha started getting angrier. "I'm talking about literally wrestling her. Like we promised!"

I was having trouble understanding what Martha was trying to say. If I knew her well enough, she always knew violence wasn't the answer to problems like this. "I thought the wrestling part of our promise meant to scare them off with words. And last time I checked, you said violence was never the answer."

"Well, since you feel that way. I'm not your friend anymore."

Martha got out of the booth and walked towards the door. Once she reached the door and opened it, she gave me one last angry look and then walked out. Tammy started laughing.

"There's my entertainment for the day," Tammy said as she flipped her hair behind her shoulder.

I wanted to say something back to Tammy, but I was utterly speechless about what had happened. Our past arguments have never gotten to the point of ending our friendship. Was she earnest when she said she was not my friend anymore? I was hoping not because Martha is the only friend I have. She is the only friend who understands what I'm going through regarding my mom, the only friend who understands me as a person, and the only friend who is like a sister to me.

I remained at the booth with my elbows on the table while putting my face into my hands. I was trying to hold back the tears as best as I could. As hard as I tried, I at least felt one or two tears go down my cheek. I wiped those tears away and took a deep breath. As I closed my eyes, I told myself I had to stay strong—not only because Tammy was here but also because of the new waitress I was training.

As I left the booth, Jenny approached me and said she was ready to return to training. As I talked to Jenny about ways to greet customers, Jenny asked me if something was wrong. I was hoping I wasn't making it too apparent that I was upset about the situation with Martha, but it turns out I was. At first, I told Jenny I didn't want to talk about it, but she kept saying to me it was okay to talk to her about the problem, and I eventually gave in.

"Well, she certainly sounds immature for her age," she said.

"I wouldn't say that about her, but you're probably right," I said. Talking to her about the situation did help me a little bit, and it helped me get through the day without thinking about it so much. "Now, the food is ready for table eleven."

As Jenny and I continued working, my cell phone started ringing. I flip opened my phone and didn't recognize the number. I initially hesitated to answer, but something told me to do so. So, I did. It turned out to be a neighbor of my mom and me on a phone number I didn't have from them. Unlike Mom, when I was doing yard work, I met one of the neighbors, and she was very nice to me. She has two kids, ages six and eight. In between high school graduation and working at the diner, I offered to babysit her kids anytime she needed me. She has my number mainly for that reason.

"Oh hey, Gayle. How is it going?" I said after Gayle mentioned it was her.

"Not good. Your house is on fire," she said.

My eyes widened, and my mouth dropped in a panic. "Oh my gosh! Is my mom out of the house?"

"Yes, she is."

"Oh my gosh! I'll get there as soon as I can!"

CHAPTER 3

The fire fully engulfed the house. There were at least three fire trucks and two police cars at the house when I got there. I was in complete shock when I saw this. As I stood outside of my car on the road, stared at the house being on fire, and watched the firefighters do what they could to take it out, I kept on thinking, how in the world did this happen? Did I do something to cause the fire? As far as I could remember, I didn't recall leaving anything on that could cause a fire.

As I kept thinking, I looked at one of the police cars and saw Mom sitting in the back seat. Wondering why she was sitting in the back of the police car, I walked up to a nearby cop talking to one of the neighbors and asked him why my mom was sitting in the back of the vehicle.

"Your Mom is under arrest for arson. It appears that she intentionally set the house on fire. We're not sure why yet, but we will investigate further on it," the officer said.

"Intentionally?!" I said, even more shocked. Sure, my mom has done stupid things while being under the influence of alcohol, but she never has gone this far.

"Yeah. One of your neighbors happened to be outside when she witnessed your mom stacking wood by the front door.

Once she finished, she lit it up, and before you knew it, the house blew up into flames," the officer said.

My hands were on my head in complete shock. I didn't know what to think. As I stood speechless, I noticed my blanket, pillow, phone charger, and clothes near the curb beside the driveway. At first glance, I was glad some of my items were not in the fire. As I got closer, I noticed a folded note with my name on it. I opened the note and read it.

Now you have no place to live. You don't deserve to live. Nobody likes you. I felt the need to burn down this house so you can live a painful, miserable life like I've lived since you were born. Love, Mom.

Tears flooded my eyes after reading that. I may be used to my mom saying horrible things to me, but she never said or done anything like this in my life. I knew I wasn't her favorite person in the world, but to say I gave her a painful and miserable life ever since I was born hit me hard. I'm sure I wasn't that much of a burden on her life, being her only child. After all, I always stayed away from her since I didn't want to be close to her alcoholic behavior.

After crying for a minute, I did my best to wipe the tears from my eyes, which was nearly impossible. I walked back to the officer along with my belongings and explained what I just found. The officer took the note from me and asked me if there was anything else he needed to know about my mom. I explained all that I could to him about her being an alcoholic and her being verbally abusive towards me. Then the officer gave me a business card to the police station in case I had more information for them regarding my mom, and I regathered my things and walked to my car.

Walking to my car, I realized I had nowhere to stay. I could stay at Martha's if we were friends, but since we're not on good terms right now, that is not happening. I couldn't think of any other friends I had. I thought about asking Gayle if I could stay at her place, but I thought I shouldn't since she already had two kids to care for. I didn't want to put extra pressure on her.

Plus, I'm not one to ask people for help even though I need it. If someone offered me help, I would accept it when needed. When I don't have help provided to me, I don't bother asking for it. I'm always scared of how the response will be. Whenever I needed help with my homework. Mom's reaction would always be, 'People who ask for help are dumb and useless' or 'Why should I help someone as dumb as you?' Getting those responses made me scared to ask for help, no matter what I needed help with. Even as serious as this issue is, I am afraid to ask for help.

I put my belongings into the backseat of my car and felt tears streaming down my face. Constantly thinking about where I'd stay, I continued watching the firefighters spraying water hoses toward the house as the house continued to blow up in flames.

Although the thought of no place to stay continued to take over my mind, I felt like the memories of horror in that house were burning down, and I could finally move on from them. It won't be the easiest thing to do, and I'm sure Mom's words will continue to haunt me daily, but at least I don't have to look at that house again once I drive away.

I got in the driver's seat of my car and gripped the steering wheel as I turned on the ignition. I took a deep breath and realized that I would be sleeping in my car. I could not think of anywhere else to stay, and I did not want to spend money on a hotel.

I hear the music playing, put the car in drive, and slowly drive off as I take a final look at the house, which I now see as a haunting memory.

Suddenly, I realized I had no hygiene products with my belongings. After noticing, I drove to the store and grabbed cheap travel-size products. I also grabbed some snacks and water there, so I didn't end up hungry. I can ask Barbara if I can have some meals at the diner for a discounted price so I can at least get something more than just a snack here and there until I get things together. Barbara is very understanding, but I hope she understands enough to help me.

Now, let's return to the major problem: where should I park my car and sleep?

The only place I can think of is the diner's parking lot, so I know I will be less likely to get noticed by cops. I hope Barbara is alright with me doing this until I get my place.

As the sun shined through my car window the following day, I woke up in so much pain. I lay in the back seat of my car, my head on my pillow and my blanket over my body. I lay on my back the entire night, slightly curved because the backseat wasn't big enough for me to move around. My back was hurting from that position. My arms also hurt because I laid my head on them for more support, along with the pillow.

I slowly got myself sitting up and rubbed my eyes to wake up. As I did that, I noticed Barbara at the diner's front door, getting ready to unlock the door. It was time for me to get out of the car as quickly as possible and speak to Barbara about my situation, even though it would probably hurt slightly.

"Morning, Barbara!" I said as I got out of my car.

Morning, Elizabeth. What are you doing here so early?" Barbara said.

"As you probably remember, my house was on fire yesterday. My Mom got arrested, and the house was completely damaged. Having no place to stay, I slept in my car here. By any chance, can I freshen up here and maybe have some breakfast at a discounted price, please?"

"I'm sorry to hear that happened, Elizabeth. Go ahead and get yourself ready. One of the cooks will be here in thirty minutes so I'll tell him what you want to eat. What would you like?"

"I'll just have a couple of pieces of wheat toast with jelly on the side and a glass of orange juice. How much will it cost?"

"Nothing."

"You sure?"

"Yes, I'm sure."

"Thank you, Barbara. Is it okay to sleep in my car here until I get a place to live?"

"Of course."

"Thank you. Thank you very much, Barbara."

As Barbara opened the door to the diner, she let me go in, and I walked straight to the bathroom.

When I opened the bathroom door, I saw the purple flower wallpaper and inhaled the scent of a flowery air freshener. I have always enjoyed the smell of flowers and appreciate how they look.

When I turned my head and looked at the mirror in the bathroom, I saw my hair was a huge mess. My hair looked like it got struck by lightning. I hate dealing with hair like that, especially when I don't have the proper hair products to maintain it. But what choice did I have? I got my brush out of the store bag and started brushing away. As expected, I pulled the brush through my hair the first time, and it got stuck in a hair knot. Hair knots are the worst, especially when they are impossible to get out of my hair.

It took some time to get knot after knot out of my hair, but I eventually got it to where I could put it into a messy bun. I brushed my teeth, put on some deodorant, and changed clothes. I may have only a few sets of clothes at this time, but if there is one thing I do not like, it's wearing the same clothes two days in the same week. I hope to get some tip money daily to wash my clothes I'm not wearing at least once a week.

I take one last look in the mirror to ensure I'm presentable enough for a day at work and then gather my things into my plastic store bag. After collecting my belongings, I head to the main dining area and see my toast and juice sitting at a table close to the kitchen.

After I finished my toast and juice, it was time for the diner to open.

Lunchtime is always busy at the diner. Customers nearly filled all tables. All of us were working our butts off. This part of my shift was the time of day when I got the most tips.

As I cleaned one of my tables, I noticed Martha walking into the diner with a guy I hadn't met before. The guy was tall, looked thin yet a bit muscular, and had perfectly combed blonde hair. Seeing Martha with a guy like that made me jealous, especially since we're not friends. I wish I had some guy who was as good-looking in my life, especially with the situation I'm in currently. If I had a guy like that, I would have a place to sleep and someone to support me during this emotionally difficult time. But sadly, I don't. So, I have to deal with it myself.

I saw Martha and the guy sitting at a table that happened to be one of my tables. I thought it would be the perfect chance to discuss the argument ordeal with Martha. I hope our friendship isn't ruined for good because Martha is like a sister to me, and I can't imagine my life without her as my best friend. She is, after all, the only person who understands me and is always there for me when I'm having problems with my life. No one can understand me like she does.

After getting to the table, I asked Martha and her friend, "Hello, can I get you two something to drink?"

"Two colas and a new waiter," Martha said, giving me an angry look while stroking her black hair behind her ear.

"I'm sorry?"

"A new waiter, please? Because I don't like to have you as a waiter."

"But this is my table, and I'd be happy to serve you."

"We'll have two colas, please," Martha's friend said. |

I left the table to grab the colas for them. As I was doing that, I saw Martha's friend head towards the restroom. I thought that this was the time to talk to Martha.

"Here are your colas. And now I'm going to sit down," I said after returning to Martha's table. As I sat down, Martha looked at me blankly yet angry. "Now, Martha, before you say anything, please tell me exactly why you're mad at me?"

"I felt like you didn't have my back when your co-waitress was mean to me," Martha said.

"Why exactly did you feel like that? I tried to get her to leave us alone, but she wouldn't listen."

"You didn't wrestle her to the ground."

"That was part of our promise as a joke. At least, I thought it was. You know as well as I know that violence doesn't solve anything."

Martha looked down for a second as if she was thinking of something. "True. We were twelve when we started that promise."

"Exactly. And now we're mature enough to know that violence isn't the answer. Right?"

"Yeah, I guess. When we tell each other 'Wrestle that person to the ground,' we mean to wrestle with words," Martha started to laugh slightly.

"Yeah, like cursing them out until they're on the ground," I started to laugh.

"I'm sorry I overreacted, Elizabeth."

"I'm sorry I made you feel like I didn't have your back, Martha."

Martha and I smiled at each other. It was nice to know that our friendship was not ruined after all. I wanted to tell her about my homeless situation, but as I was about to say something, her friend came back.

"Tim, this is my best friend, Elizabeth. Elizabeth, this is Tim. Tim is my boyfriend," Martha said.

"Nice to meet you, Tim," I said while shaking his hand.

"Nice to meet you too," Tim said.

"Just so you know, Tim, if you somehow break Martha's heart, I will break your face."

Martha and I may have just talked about how we should not solve problems with violence, but I will continue to say the phrase I just said no matter what, even though, in reality, I would probably never break their face literally.

"Not to worry. I could never break Martha's heart. She's lovely, fun, and beautiful," he said.

I have only known Tim for one minute, but he seems to be a nice guy for Martha. I wanted to get to know him more to be sure he was good to Martha, but sadly, I had to return to waitress duties. I took lunch orders from Tim and Martha and then checked other tables.

While picking plates from a table, I looked at Jenny to see how she handled the job independently. She looked back at me with an angry look and slowly shook her head. She even crossed her arms. I wasn't sure why she was looking at me like that. I couldn't recall doing anything to upset her during her training yesterday. I wanted to ask Jenny about that, but it wasn't the best time.

Once I turned around with some dishes in my hands, shaking off Jenny's expression towards me, Tammy appeared out of nowhere.

"Elizabeth, stop being a sore loser and get back to work!" she said.

"Okay, I will!" I said.

After I put the dirty dishes away, I immediately walked to Barbara's office.

"Barbara, you got a minute?" I said after knocking on her door and opening it.

"Yes. What's going on, Elizabeth?" she said.

"Why did you re-hire Tammy? If you don't mind me asking."

"What are you talking about?"

"Why is Tammy working here again?"

"She's not working here again. Is she out there right now?"

"Yes."

Barbara immediately got out of her seat and went to confront Tammy. When Barbara confronted Tammy and told her to get out, Tammy got all defensive. Barbara was not playing games, however. Barbara even threatened to call the police if she wouldn't leave.

Eventually, Tammy gave up and headed for the door. I opened the front door for her with a smile on my face.

"There's my entertainment for the day," I said mockingly. I hope this will be the last time I see her in this diner. Or anywhere.

Before Barbara returned to her office, she informed me that I was welcome to have a free lunch today. I wasn't expecting that. I thought I had to survive with a snack from the store.

After I thanked her, Barbara went back to her office, and I went to place my lunch order.

It was closing time at the diner, and I ensured I had everything as I walked out the door to my car. As I got my phone out, I thought about calling Martha and seeing if I could stay at her place instead of sleeping in my car again. Now that Martha and I were good again, I was sure she would help me.

I checked behind me as I got halfway to my car and ensured someone else was in the diner to lock up. As I did, Jenny approached me and gave me an angry look.

"I can't believe you! You should be ashamed of yourself," Jenny said as she followed me.

"For what?" I said.

"For being friends with Martha again!"

When Jenny mentioned Martha's name like that, I got angry with her and wanted to get away from her. " If you're mad at me, why are you following me?"

"I'm trying to understand why you decided to befriend Martha after what she did to you."

I got to my car and turned around to face Jenny. During the brief pause, I was starting to think maybe Jenny was not the forgiving type. I believe in forgiving people as long as they didn't do something violent or I felt they didn't deserve a second chance. I started to think Jenny didn't deserve a second chance because of how she talked about my best friend. "You know what? You make a good point. You should leave people who don't treat you right." Then I raised my tone, "And I'm looking at the perfect example!" After saying that, I got into my car and shut the door on her even though she was still talking.

"Gee! I thought you were smarter than that!"

"Go away!"

"See? Now you want to act crazy like Martha."

"Crazy? You haven't personally met her. We have been best friends for ten years. We apologized to each other for the disagreement."

"You idiot! You don't know what you're getting yourself into! Even though we work together, we're no longer friends from this day forward."

Jenny walked away as I finished typing a text to Martha. Should I feel sad about losing a friend like that? I had no problem losing Jenny as a friend since I'd only known her for a couple of days. Also, I'm not too fond of the fact that she got upset about me and Martha being friends again. I would think that someone like her would be happy for us. Jenny's friendship wasn't a total loss like Martha's would have been if we had not made up.

Martha responded to my text, saying I could stay as long as needed. It was a wonderful feeling knowing that I had someone who was always there for me to help, no matter the situation. I felt relieved that I finally had a place to stay. Hopefully, I don't make her feel like I'm taking up too much space, and I don't get on her nerves.

CHAPTER 4

Martha lived in a one-bedroom apartment Her utilities, excluding electricity and gas, are included with her rent. Her lease states that she can have a guest stay as long as the landlord knows. A fee would be added to the rent bill if the guest stays for over a month. Martha says she is not worried about that fee. If I had to stay at her place for over a month, she would pay for it with no problem. However, I felt terrible that Martha would have to pay extra just for me to be there. I'm hoping I get my situation together soon.

Once I brought my belongings inside Martha's apartment, Martha and I sat on the couch in her living room and started catching up. While catching up, we enjoyed a cheese and pepperoni pizza Martha ordered.

"So, how did you meet Tim? He seems pretty nice," I said.

"I met him while I was swimming in the pool here. He also lives in this apartment complex," Martha said. "I was floating in the pool, and he came to me out of nowhere and complimented me. Then we started chatting, went on a couple of dates, and now here we are a couple of weeks later."

"That's nice. I wish I could find a boyfriend. Especially one as nice looking as yours."

"You could if you lived in an apartment here and swam in the pool. I'm sure there are plenty of single guys living here."

"Yeah, maybe. I wouldn't mind living close to my best friend, too."

"Totally! Why did you suddenly have to move out of your mom's house?"

I told Martha the story regarding Mom setting the house on fire. As I did, Martha's eyes widened. They kept widening as I gave more details about what happened.

"Wow! That's crazy!" Martha said.

"I know, right!" I said.

"I'm so sorry you have to deal with this," Martha started rubbing my back.

"It's hard. But I think living here will be a fresh start."

"Yeah. And before you know it, you'll have that boyfriend you've always wanted."

"I'll see the landlord tomorrow since I'm not working. I hope they have an apartment available so I have one less thing to worry about in my situation."

"I hope all goes well with that."

After finishing the pizza, Martha and I watched TV until it was time for bed. Martha said that I could sleep on the couch. I wasn't going to complain about that. It was more comfortable than lying in the back seat of my car.

"What was your previous address?" said the landlord of Martha's apartment complex.

I gave the landlord, Linda Sanana, all the information she needed for an apartment. She said an apartment was available, but it was a studio apartment. That didn't bother me because I needed a place to live as soon as possible.

"Everything looks good here. I need a four-hundred-dollar deposit, and you should be all good to go," Linda said.

I initially hesitated because that was all the money I had saved for the past few years. I didn't like the idea of just giving it all away in a snap. But I knew I had no choice because it was vital for me to have some place to live. I wrote out a check for the deposit and handed it to Linda.

"Thank you. Here's your key. Your apartment number is forty-two. Your rent is due on the first of each month. Your rent includes utilities except for electricity and gas. Do you have any questions?" Linda said.

"No, I don't," I said.

"Okay. Here's a copy of your lease. Congrats on your new apartment, Elizabeth."

"Thank you."

After walking out of the leasing office, I stared at the key to my apartment. I couldn't help but feel excited to have a key to my very own place finally. It is one of the greatest feelings I have ever experienced. I don't have to worry about my mom reacting to things. I can finally do what I want to do without her criticizing me.

Five buildings were on the property, including the building where the leasing office. Each building has two levels. The apartments have doors for each apartment on the outside. The main building is smaller than the others, but it has a fitness center, an area for people to gather, and an indoor pool. My building was the fourth one down from the main building, just like Martha's. It may be a walk from the main building to the apartment, but I was willing to walk on a nice day like today.

I went straight to my new apartment, and once I opened the door, I fell in love with it. The walls were white and the flooring was half-tan carpet and half-tan tiles. The carpet covered the entire apartment from the door to the halfway mark. There was also a small closet in the carpeted area.

After the halfway mark, the tiles covered the rest of the flooring. The kitchen has a wall that covers part of the kitchen but has an opening to walk through. Once in the kitchen, you would see the stove, sink, counter, and a doorway to the bathroom. The bathroom had the same tiles as the kitchen. It had a white granite sink counter and a white toilet. The bathroom only had a walk-in shower. The shower did, however, have a sliding door instead of a shower curtain.

I couldn't help but smile so big. It didn't matter to me how small it was; I was so in love with it. I felt the need to celebrate somehow. But before that, I thought I had to set up things like electricity and gas.

I realized my belongings were still at Martha's as I got the electric and gas going. Thankfully, she gave me her key while she went to work. She figured I would go in and out today since I was not working, so she gave me her key.

As I was about to leave the apartment and go to Martha's apartment, my phone rang. I didn't recognize the number but answered it anyway, thinking it was the landlord.

"Hello?" I answered.

"Elizabeth! I hear you're living at the Romando apartments," said the caller. I immediately recognized the voice and was shocked.

"Rita Sanana? From high school?"

"The one and only."

"How did you get this number?"

"From my sister, Linda. Also known as your landlord!"

"And why did you get my number from her?"

"Because she knew you and I were great friends in high school. She also knows I've been trying to find you since graduation."

"I don't remember being friends with you."

"Sounds like you're the same idiot you were in high school!"

Rita then hung up.

Rita and I met in high school. She was one of the most popular girls in school. In her junior and senior years, she was head cheerleader and prom queen and got whatever she wanted. With her long, straight red hair, perfect figure, and expensive clothes, I was jealous of her.

She would always tease me and Martha. However, out of me and Martha, I was her primary target because for some reason, she enjoyed seeing me miserable compared to her happy lifestyle.

Her sister, Linda, is older by a couple of years. While Linda is the landlord of the Romando apartments, Rita works as a housekeeper at a local hotel.

I hoped that high school graduation would be the last time I saw or heard from her again, but I was wrong.

After staring at the phone in shock for a few seconds, I texted Martha, telling her I had gotten the apartment and which one I lived in. Once I sent that, I started walking towards Martha's apartment to gather my things.

While walking towards her apartment, I get a response from Martha saying she will stop by the apartment after she gets off work.

CHAPTER 5

After getting my stuff back from Martha's, I started organizing my things well, even though there was little to manage. Since I didn't have a bed, the best thing I could do was arrange my blanket and pillow into a bed. I may be sleeping on the carpeted floor for some time, but I'm sure I'll survive. If I make enough tips in the next few weeks. I'll buy a small bed or couch—whatever I can find cheap and quick.

Once that was all set up, I put the few clothes I'd worn on the ground in the little closet to remind myself that they needed washing. I hung the clothes I had yet to wear around the rack in the little closet since I had no hangers.

While I put my hygiene stuff away, I heard a knock at the front door. I went to check through the peephole and saw that it was Martha. I opened the door and saw Martha holding a plastic bag in her hand with stuff I could not see clearly.

"What do you have there?" I said after we said our hellos.

"It's a present for you," Martha said.

"Aw, thank you, Martha. You didn't have to get me anything."

After she handed over the bag, I opened it. Inside was a light blue one-piece swimsuit with a sunflower design. Along with that was a pink and orange beach towel with a seashell design. I wasn't expecting a gift from her, but I thought that was very sweet of her.

"This is awesome, Martha! Thank you!" I said as I hugged her.

"Of course, Elizabeth. Now let's go celebrate your new apartment with a swim," Martha said.

"For sure!"

"I will grab my swimsuit and then meet you at the pool. Can I get my key back?"

After giving Martha her apartment key, I ensured I had the swimsuit and towel in the bag. Seeing that I had everything I needed, I walked out of my apartment.

Once I left my apartment, I started walking to the leasing building.

The in-ground pool is thirty by ten feet. There is also an eight-foot by eight-foot in-ground jacuzzi. The pool had a good number of people in it.

I went to the restroom and changed into my swimsuit. The swimsuit fit just right, and when I looked in the mirror, I thought it looked good on me.

Grabbing my clothes and towel, I walked out of the restroom and was ready to swim. I looked to see if Martha had shown up yet but did not see her anywhere. I figured while waiting for her, I could get a head start and get into the pool.

I stepped into the pool, and the water felt so warm. I started to float on my back after I got in. As I floated around, some random guy with a full head of short brown hair approached me.

"Hey. I like your swimsuit," the guy said.

"Thanks. My best friend got it for me as a gift. I just moved here," I said.

"Well, welcome to the Romando Apartments. I'm Matt," Matt held out his hand.

"I'm Elizabeth," I grabbed his hand and shook it.

Matt and I continued talking while leaning against the edge of the pool.

Martha eventually came with her swimsuit on and jumped into the pool once she saw me. I introduced Matt to Martha, and we talked and played pool games. Matt seemed to be fun and friendly.

As Matt said he had to leave, he said, "Elizabeth, would you like to go out for dinner tonight?"

"Yeah. That would be great," I responded.

"Awesome! Meet me in the parking lot at six tonight near this building."

As Matt exited the pool and headed towards the restroom, Martha and I looked at each other excitedly. We started hugging and expressing our excitement about me getting a date. As we continued showing our excitement, Linda walked near the pool and called my name while motioning me to approach her.

"Yes, Linda?" I said.

"Why were you mean to my sister?" Linda said.

"I don't recall being mean to her. She said we were friends in high school, but that never happened. Is she really that stupid?"

"What did you just say?"

"All I asked was if she was stupid."

"I'll be right back."

My face turned as hot as a jalapeno pepper. I had no idea why I had just said that to Linda. Yes, I think Rita is stupid, but I had no idea why I let that come out of my mouth to my landlord, who is also Rita's sister. I felt so dumb and worried. I was afraid about what Linda would do with my lease now that I had just said that. I truly hoped I wasn't about to lose my new apartment the same day I got it.

Linda has always been the sister who would have her sister's back no matter what. Although she and Rita have had their fair share of disagreements, Linda always had Rita's back, no matter what.

"What happened?" Martha asked as I got back in the pool.

"Linda asked me why I was mean to Rita," I said.

"Wait a minute, you mean the Rita who was such a bitch in high school? That Rita?"

'Yes. Rita called my cell phone today and said she got my number from Linda, also known as her sister."

Martha widened her eyes as I explained my phone call with Rita. She did not realize that our landlord was her sister.

"Why on earth did Linda give your number to that psycho?" she said.

"I guess Rita sweet-talked her into thinking me and Rita were best friends back in the day, which, as you and I know, is a total lie."

"I knew that bitch wouldn't change after high school."

"You know, I heard someone say that she works as a housekeeper at some hotel these days."

Martha and I started laughing, mainly because Rita was the girl who always got what she wanted in high school; we found it funny how now, all of a sudden, she has to work to get what she wants. And the fact that she is working a cleaning-type job. Knowing Rita, she probably hates that job a hundred percent.

"That's what she gets for bullying us," Martha said.

As Martha and I continued laughing, Linda returned and had Rita with her.

"Miss Elizabeth! Come here, please," Linda said.

"Yes, Linda?" I said once I got out of the pool and approached them.

"Is there something you want to say to Rita?"

As nervous as I was to answer that question, I could only say, "I don't have anything to say," because it was the truth. I had no idea why Linda had brought Rita to me except to show Rita that I was there.

"Elizabeth, I believe you owe Rita an apology. I told her about how you called her stupid."

"Linda, I did not call her stupid. I asked if she was stupid."

"Wow. As I said, the same idiot you were in high school," Rita said.

Linda looked at Rita with a confused expression, wondering why Rita had said that.

"Now, where's my fifty dollars, Linda?" Rita continued.

"What fifty dollars? And why did you talk to Elizabeth like that?" Linda said. "Because I can. And you promised me fifty dollars if I came. So where is it?"

"I don't recall offering you fifty dollars. All I said was what Elizabeth told me about you, and you said you wanted to see her in person."

"Whatever," Rita walked away after saying that while Linda stayed.

"I'm sorry she talked to you like that, Elizabeth. I never expected Rita to talk like that."

I didn't take Rita's words too personally since I'm used to her teasing me. I just blew it off and thanked Linda before I jumped back into the pool.

As Martha and I had fun swimming, I noticed that for the first time in so long, I felt like I was in a happy place other than my bedroom at Mom's house. I felt free. I felt like I could finally enjoy life and not worry about so much. For once, my life was going in the right direction.

As the evening approached, I put on my best available outfit. It was a plain light pink V-neck T-shirt and a black skirt. Martha let me borrow her black heels. Having a best friend who wears the same shoe size is excellent. Martha also lent me her makeup and some gold dangling earrings. I'm so grateful to have Martha in my life for many reasons. Letting me borrow some stuff for date night is one of them. Especially since mostly everything I had got burnt down in the house fire.

After I was all set, I walked to the parking lot near the leasing building, where Matt had said to meet, but he was nowhere to be seen. At first, I thought he would not show up like people did before on dates in high school. But then I figured he probably needed a little more time to prepare. While I continued to wait, I leaned back against the wall of the leasing building and looked toward the sky.

While making shapes of the clouds, a red jeep pulled up in front of me, and the person behind the wheel got out of the vehicle.

"Hey, Elizabeth. You look very nice tonight," Matt said as he opened the passenger door for me.

"Thanks, Matt. You look very nice yourself," I said as I blushed.

Matt wore a light blue flannel shirt, black jeans, and shiny black shoes. He also wore round framed contact glasses with metal rims.

"Thank you. Ready for dinner?" Matt said.

"I sure am," I said.

As Matt drove us to the restaurant, we got to know each other better. Matt works as an emergency medical technician and hopes to become a doctor one day. He is currently in medical school part-time. Matt decided to go into the medical field because he has always been interested in how the human body works and how it can be fixed.

After talking about his career, he asked me about mine. I was nerve us about answering that since I'm not attending college like him and because I'm a waitress. I was scared Matt would not like me anymore after I told him.

I eventually gained the courage to tell Matt where I currently work and that I'm not in college. Shockingly, he was very understanding after I told him. He gave me some ideas of careers that don't require an education, which gave me something to think about.

Matt and I arrived at an Italian restaurant a few minutes later. I've never been to the restaurant, but Matt says it is a good place.

We walked through the main entrance, and I saw a fountain in the center of the waiting area. That fountain had a statue of a mermaid sitting on it. The water flowed from under the mermaid and dropped to the fountain's center part. And like any water fountain, there were a bunch of coins from people making wishes in the center part of it.

A hostess took Matt and me to a booth. Immediately after the hostess walked away, a waitress came to our table and immediately recognized Matt.

"Matt! How are you doing?" she said as she hugged him.

"I'm good. How are you, Maria?" Matt said.

"I'm good. It's so nice to see you!" Maria flips her long and straightened dark brown hair back. "Are you on a date?"

"Yes. Could we get two colas, please?"

"Sure thing!"

Maria walked away, and I gave Matt a confused expression for a second.

"Maria's my ex-girlfriend, but we're still friends."

I'll give him points for being honest. "I see. What broke off the relationship? If you don't mind me asking."

"I went to college out of state for my Bachelor's degree. She didn't like the idea of a long-distance relationship, so we paused our relationship. We still kept in touch, though. After graduating with my Bachelor's degree, I returned to town in hopes of resuming the relationship. In the end, she found someone else. So, we agreed just to be friends."

"I'm sorry that didn't work out as you hoped." I may say that to him, but I don't mean it. After all, if it hadn't happened the way it did, I would never have met Matt and had this night with him.

Matt shrugged, "Everything happens for a reason."

Maria brought our colas while Matt and I continued talking. As she handed over my drink, she gave me an angry look. I was unsure why she did that, but I brushed it off, thinking I was being paranoid. I figured I was overthinking it because it was Matt's ex-girlfriend.

Maria took our orders and then walked away.

Matt and I continued talking. As we were talking, I noticed Maria looking at me, angry again. After seeing it a couple more times, I realized I was not being paranoid; she was looking at me angrily. Was Maria jealous that I was with Matt? Or is she making sure I was a good girl for Matt? I tried not to let it get to me, even though it drove me crazy. But I wanted to make sure I enjoyed this night. Tonight is my first date in so long, after all. Matt started telling me about his childhood. He says he had a decent childhood until he was eight years old.

When Matt was eight, his mom became ill with lung cancer. She battled the cancer for two years, going through chemotherapy and other treatments. Unfortunately, she lost that battle.

During the two years that his mom was in hospitals, Matt would stay in those hospitals with his mom when he wasn't in school. While with his mom, he watched doctors and nurses do their jobs, which interested him in how the human body works. He also said that when he becomes a doctor, he plans to find a cure for lung cancer.

I found Matt impressive so far. It was amazing to see how he is reaching career goals and how he plans to turn his challenging experience of losing his mom into something positive for others who battle the same. I've never met a guy as driven as Matt.

I started to tell Matt about my childhood. It wasn't easy to speak about, but since he told me about his heartbreaking childhood, I figured I should tell him about my rough childhood.

"I can tell you're a brave woman. If I were to go through that, I would be scared to be on my own," Matt said after I finished telling him about my childhood.

"I was scared at first. But when my mom burnt the house down, I had no other choice but to face that fear. Now I'm happy to be on my own."

While Matt and I were still talking, our food came. Once again, Maria looked at me angrily. I was growing more concerned because of how often she looked at me like that.

After she set our food on the table. Matt thanked her, and she smiled back at him. As she started walking away, she stopped for a second at a spot where Matt couldn't see her. Maria gave me the same angry look and slowly shook her head. Another second later, she walked away.

Once Maria disappeared from our area, I immediately asked Matt if Maria tended to be angry. He responded, "No. Not at all. She is a very nice person." I wanted to believe Matt even though I had doubts.

I enjoyed the food. Even though I was getting full, I couldn't stop eating. Matt was done with his plate before I finished mine.

"I must say," I said, "this food is quite delicious."

"I knew you would like it," Matt said.

After I finished eating, we got our bill, and Matt went to pay for it. As I was grabbing my things to get ready to go, Maria came to the table. And as I expected, she had an angry look on her face.

"What's your name?" Maria said.

"Elizabeth," I said.

"Let's get one thing straight, Elizabeth. Matt belongs with me and not you."

"Aren't you with someone else?"

"Not anymore. It seems like fate is bringing Matt and me together again, but you're getting in the way. So do me a favor and stop trying to steal Matt from me." Maria grabbed the empty plates from the table and walked away after saying that. Now I know for sure I was not overthinking Maria.

I couldn't stop thinking about Maria's words during the ride home. I kept trying to think of the fun parts of tonight, but that wasn't helping. I tried having some conversations with Matt to distract myself from the thoughts.

We arrived back at the Romando apartments and got out of the jeep. Matt then walked me to my apartment. I offered him to come in, but he said he had to get sleep for work the next day.

Matt and I exchanged phone numbers and then hugged each other.

After Matt said goodnight, he started walking towards his apartment.

I wish the night didn't have to end so quickly. I had a great time with Matt. I hope we can hang out again soon.

As the night went on, I laid under my blanket on the carpeted floor of my apartment. I couldn't stop thinking about Matt. I kept thinking about how fun it was to be with him. Judging from the date I had with him, Matt seemed very sweet. He also seemed so bright. Of course, he was charming with his glasses and nice brown hair. If only I could rub my fingers through that nice hair right now.

It may be too early to tell, but I can see Matt as a future boyfriend of mine. I sure hope he feels the same way.

CHAPTER 6

Waking up in my apartment felt like a dream at first. It's still hard to believe I'm living in my apartment. Of course, lying on the floor wasn't the most comfortable way to sleep, but I could handle it. It is more comfortable than sleeping in my car, that's for sure.

As I stretched out my arms and legs and tried to wake myself up, I grabbed my phone, charging not too far from me. On my phone, I found a text message from Matt. Just seeing his name on my phone made my heart skip a beat. The message stated, 'Had a wonderful time last night! Hope we can hang out again tonight.' Seeing him write that put a big smile on my face. It was an excellent thing to wake up to.

I read the message a dozen more times because I couldn't help but enjoy the idea that he wanted to hang out again. I couldn't wait!

As I reread the message, I glanced at the clock on my phone and realized it was about time for work. I immediately got up and prepared myself for work.

I walked into work promptly and saw Jenny conducting waitress duties at her tables. After I clocked in, I went up to Jenny to talk to her about what happened the other night. Although her saying we weren't friends didn't affect me, I just wanted to understand why she was mad that I was friends with Martha again. To me, it didn't make any sense.

"Jenny, can we talk about the other night?" I said.

"Why would I talk to a stupid girl named Elizabeth?" Jenny said in an angry tone.

"I don't understand why you're mad at me for being friends with Martha. Can't we accept how things are and be friends?"

"I said this once before, and now I'll say it again. Even though we work together, we're no longer friends from this day forward."

Jenny put her hand toward my face as if she wanted me to talk to the hand instead of her and then went back to work. At that point, I could only shake my head and roll my eyes at how she acted. She must be a jealous type of person or something.

I started waiting tables as the breakfast rush began, trying my best not to think about what Jenny said to me. While I was working, Matt walked into the diner, and I couldn't help but smile. He looked very handsome in his EMT uniform.

"Table for two, please," Matt said in a cute tone.

I looked around but didn't see anybody with him. "Waiting for someone?" I said.

"No. She is already here and standing right in front of me."

I blushed and chuckled a little bit. I thought that response was cute. "I will take you to a seat and get myself ready for a small break."

After sitting Matt at one of my tables, I informed another waitress I was taking a short break and grabbed a couple of colas for Matt and me.

"I saw your text this morning. I would be up for hanging out again tonight," I said once I sat across from Matt.

"I'm glad to hear that. I was thinking about going out to dinner again tonight and then going for a swim after that. What do you think?" Matt said.

"That sounds like fun."

"Cool. I'll meet you at your apartment after I get off work."

Matt and I discussed what time we'd see each other, and then I returned to work after taking his breakfast order. I checked the kitchen for orders and put in Matt's order afterward, and then I went to check on my other tables. While checking my other tables, I noticed someone sitting with Matt. I went to his table and saw it was Maria. My question is, did she know Matt was here? Or is it that small of a world?

"Hey, Maria. Nice to see you again," I said as I tried to hide my anger towards her. "Can I get you something to drink?"

"I'll have water, please," Maria said as I handed her a menu. At first, she smiled at me. However, when Matt looked out the window, Maria looked at me angrily and mouthed something like she was saying, 'He's mine.' In response, I gave Maria a mean look and walked away.

As I grabbed Maria's water, I kept looking toward Matt's table to see what Maria was up to. Her constantly saying Matt belongs with her and giving me mean stares made me increasingly suspicious.

"Are you ready to order?" I said to Maria once I gave her the water.

"I won't be ordering anything. Thank you, though," Maria said.

I overheard their conversation as I went to the table behind those two to clean it.

"Isn't it obvious. Matt? Fate brought us to where we would run into each other at the restaurant because we belong together," Maria said.

"But you broke up with me when I went out of state. When I came back, you were with someone else," Matt said.

"Why does that matter? I can't do a long-distance relationship, and I got lonely. I'm no longer with that guy; fate is bringing us back together. Matt, I want to live the rest of my life with you."

"I think we're better off just staying friends. I'm sorry, Maria."

That gave me a sigh of relief. Hopefully, Maria will get over the pain.

Maria made an angry look at Matt. "You will regret this one day!"

Maria got out of her seat and stormed out of the restaurant. Hopefully, Maria will stop interfering with Matt and me from now on.

Matt's food was ready to be served. After I took the food to his table, Martha walked into the restaurant.

I told Martha that Matt was here having breakfast, and she asked if she could sit with him. I escorted her to Matt's table and asked Matt if he was okay with her sitting with him. Matt said he didn't mind.

Martha, your typical caring best friend, asked Matt about his previous relationships. When Matt brought up Maria's name, Martha began questioning Matt more about her.

"Maria Frichmen? You don't mean the Maria Frichmen who recently got arrested for attempted murder, do you?" Martha said.

"Yes, I mean her. But she was falsely accused," Matt said.

"What's the matter with you? Remaining friends with a possible killer like her."

"She's not a possible killer. She is a wonderful and caring person. She wouldn't hurt a soul."

According to Martha, Maria Frichmen got arrested about a week ago for being suspected of attempted murder. She supposedly stabbed a woman a couple of times in her arm and on her side just above her hip. Her ex-lover, before Matt returned from college, cheated on Maria with that woman. Maria thought stabbing her was the best revenge there was. Maria also hoped that if the woman died, the guy would get back to dating Maria. That woman, however, survived the attack.

Police considered Maria the prime suspect after they questioned her ex-lover. Her ex-lover mentioned to police that Maria made numerous attempts to get back together with him. When the attempts failed, she started getting back at him. Some examples of getting back at him include slashing his tires, sending threatening messages to him and the woman, and hacking into his email account to send threatening or embarrassing messages to his contacts, acting like they got sent from him. When Maria was complete with her revenge on him, she met a new guy and dated him until she got taken into custody for the attempted murder of the woman. Maria is currently released on bond and is awaiting trial.

Matt never saw a mean side of Maria when they were dating, which is why he keeps defending her and believing that they are falsely accusing her of that crime.

"I would still be careful and watch out for her," Martha said. "For all we know, Elizabeth could be her next victim."

"I've known her for a long time. She is in no way a killer, and she won't go after Elizabeth," Matt said.

"Be sure to take care of Elizabeth and don't do anything to upset her. If you do, you will see my dark side."

Between working around my tables, I visit Martha and Matt to see how things are going. Sometimes, I'll even join in on their conversations.

At one point, while talking with them, Jenny approached me.

"What do you want, Jenny?" I said.

"Maybe you'd better get working on my tables because I'm leaving," Jenny said.

"Didn't Barbara call someone to come in and take your spot?"

"She did. But you should do it since you are just chilling here with your dumb friends."

"First off, my friends are not dumb. You are! Second, I shall confirm with Barbara about working your tables."

I walked to Barbara's office, and Jenny followed me. I knocked on Barbara's door and went in. I started telling Barbara what Jenny just told me.

While explaining to Barbara what happened, Jenny joined in and tried to talk over me, explaining her side of the story. Jenny and I kept talking over each other to the point where Barbara had to tell us to be quiet. She made us speak one at a time. Once we told our stories, Barbara informed Jenny that she was not the boss and couldn't tell me what to do. Barbara also said that I only work at my tables.

I gave Jenny the 'I told you so' smirk, and she looked angry. She didn't like the fact that it didn't go her way. Without saying anything, she stormed out of Barbara's office and left the restaurant.

I then went back to work and checked on Matt and Martha, but they were nowhere to be seen. I looked around the restaurant and did not see them anywhere.

I noticed a note on the table along with a five-dollar bill. The note said, 'Off to work. See you tonight. Love Matt.' I thought it was nice of him to leave a note and not leave me wondering why he left. I wasn't expecting a tip from him, but leaving one for me was also sweet.

As for Martha, I figured she had other things to do or had to go to work herself. So, I decided not to worry about that and started cleaning up the table.

While cleaning the table, I heard a big crashing sound outside the restaurant. There appeared to be a car accident right on the edge of the diner driveway. The crash looked like a very serious one. A black Nissan Altima T-boned into a red Chevy Impala.

Everybody in the diner kept looking outside to see what was going on. Some people called 911, while others took pictures with their phones. I wanted to look closer to see if everything was okay and if Matt was assisting, but I had to keep working.

Three police cars, two ambulances, and a firetruck were at the scene. The lane where the accident occurred was closed, causing traffic to get backed up. First responders took both drivers involved into the ambulances and taken to the nearby hospital. The roads cleared up an hour and a half later.

As the day went on, there were moments when the shift was hectic and moments when it was slow.

CHAPTER 7

There was a knock at my door as I put on some earrings Martha let me borrow. I felt butterflies in my tummy, believing Matt was at the door. I was so excited to go on this second date with Matt. I was a little nervous but more excited than anything.

Since Matt told me we were going swimming after we ate, I just put on some jeans and a cute reddish shirt. I felt like I needed to put on some makeup, at least to look pretty enough for Matt, but at the same time, I didn't want mascara to run down my eyes when I jumped into the pool later. All I could do was hope that even without makeup, I still looked good enough for Matt to where he wouldn't leave me.

I walked up to the door and took a deep breath to be ready to see Matt and not look nervous. As I predicted, it was Matt. He was wearing blue jeans and a turquoise polo shirt. Although the outfit was simple, I still thought he was cute.

"Ready for tonight, Elizabeth?" Matt said.

"I sure am. Matt. Are you ready?" I said.

"Of course."

Matt held out his hand like he was asking me to hold his hand. My heart skipped a beat seeing that happen. I put my hand on his hand, and our fingers interlocked. My heart then melted, and I couldn't stop smiling.

Once I locked my apartment door. Matt and I started walking toward the parking lot until I noticed a woman carrying a box toward the apartment right next to mine. She had shoulder-length black hair and big round contact glasses. Seeing that we would be neighbors from the look of it, I decided to say hi to her.

"Hi, I'm Elizabeth. Are you moving in?" I said.

The woman stopped and turned to face me, giving me an angry look. "Hey, Elizabeth. I'm Tiffany, and I don't want you anywhere near my apartment. Are we clear?" she said in an angry tone.

"Uhh...Okay?"

Looking at her confused, I turned around and returned to holding Matt's hand. As Matt and I walked to the parking lot, I couldn't help but wonder: Why was Tiffany quick to say she didn't want me near her apartment even though she hadn't met me?

We arrived at a Chinese restaurant near the apartment complex, and the hostess took us to our table. As we reached our table, I looked toward the back of the restaurant and saw Maria sitting at a table. She was wearing a brown trench coat and a brown hat as if she were Sherlock Holmes. She gave me a mean stare as I sat down. Matt noticed how I kept looking in that direction.

"What are you looking at, Elizabeth?" Matt said.

"I think I see Maria in the back over there," I said as I pointed towards Maria.

Matt looked at where I was pointing, but Maria just happened to be looking down to where her face wasn't showing. "That does kind of look like her, but it's most likely not her."

"You're sure she's not a stalker?"

"Nah. Like I told your friend. I've known her for years; she is very nice and caring. Maria wouldn't stalk anyone." Matt grabs my hand across the table. "You have nothing to worry about."

I was guessing he could see worry in my face, which embarrassed me because I didn't want him to think I was one to worry too much. I smiled at him and didn't say anything because although he said that, I was worried about what Maria was up to, especially after how she had acted at the diner towards Matt earlier. And I'm ninety-nine-point-nine percent sure that the person sitting in the back is indeed Maria. However, I didn't want tonight to get ruined, so I tried to focus on that even though it was nearly impossible.

After Matt and I ordered our food, we continued getting to know each other better. The more I talked to Matt, the more I felt like he was a perfect match for me. I could see a future with him. I was hoping he felt the same way about me.

While Matt and I kept talking, I occasionally glanced over toward Maria without making it noticeable. When I looked at her, Maria would look toward me or her cell phone.

At one point. Matt and I were talking about our hobbies. Matt likes to travel, play video games, and swim. I've never been able to travel or play video games before. Matt and I may be able to do them together someday.

I don't have many hobbies myself. My only hobby outside of writing and drawing is swimming, thanks to a daycare program my mom kept me at throughout elementary school. Whenever I was not in school (after 3 pm Monday through Friday, during summer, on the weekends, and on no-school days that were not holidays). Mom would keep me there until they were closed at night so Mom could have more alone time outside of school hours even though she was home alone most of the day while I was in school. Their program was fun, especially since I wasn't with my mom.

The daycare had a built-in pool, a gymnasium, and classrooms. On weekends, the daycare scheduled swimming. They would start us with specific swimming techniques or have us play some swimming sport for one hour, and then they would give us free time to play in the pool for thirty minutes.

Most of the time during the days there, we would do stuff in the classrooms, such as specific worksheets, reading, or doing whatever the daycare worker told us to do. We would also go to the gymnasium for sports and other exercise games that would last about an hour. We would get breakfast and lunch if we were there in the morning and afternoon. Because the daycare closed at 7 pm, they did not serve dinner. They only served snacks to us a couple of times a day. Mom usually picked me up at 6:50 pm on average. Every minute she could get without me, she would do what she could to get it.

Once I reached junior high school, Mom couldn't send me to daycare anymore because of the age limit. Whenever there was no school or school ended for the day, I would go home and be in my room most of the time because I didn't want to be around Mom, knowing she would have something mean to say about me. I would only leave my room for the bathroom, to eat, or if I needed something from her. That all changed when I started babysitting for the neighbor's kids and then when I started working at the diner.

In my spare time, I would try different hobbies in my room. I tried puzzles, painting sets, knitting, and so on. Whenever I tried a new hobby, Mom would notice how I was having fun and then consider that hobby trash. With that, she would throw away those hobbies. She would then say, 'Don't do that again!' You could say Mom did not like seeing me happy.

When I get bored or need to distract myself nowadays (where swimming isn't an option), I play games on my phone or listen to music in my car. Of course, maybe now that'll change, and I'll soon find a hobby since I no longer have to worry about Mom's thoughts. It sure felt great to be free from that home.

After I told Matt I had never traveled, he started talking about places he had been to. He also mentioned that he planned to visit Las Vegas this coming week.

"Maybe one day we can both travel to different places together. I think it would be nice to see different things worldwide," I said.

"Definitely!" Matt said with a smile as if he was thinking of a good idea.

I chuckled at that face quietly. "What are you thinking about, Matt?"

"We could go to Las Vegas together if you want."

My eyes widened in shock. I couldn't believe Matt was offering that to me. No one has ever offered me something like that before. "Really?" I started smiling from ear to ear as I began talking. But then I realized I was broke and couldn't afford to have fun like that. My smile then disappeared because of that. "That would be awesome, but I don't have any money."

"No need to worry about that. I've got you covered."

"Are you sure? I feel bad that you would have to pay for everything."

"Hey, isn't it the guy's job to pay for the girl's way into things?"

I giggled. "Yeah. That's what people say in most relationships."

"So, when are your days off? I can put vacation time on the day if I have to."

I told Matt when my days off were, which were in a couple of days, and he said those days would work well for the trip. I was shocked that he accepted those days because they were so close, but I was more excited than anything. Matt said we would leave early in the morning since it was a two-hour drive to Las Vegas from Bay City. That was very sweet of Matt. I never thought I would find a guy that is this sweet. Every guy

I have ever met was nothing but a jerk. From my dad to bullies in school, there was never a nice guy to me.

Matt and I continued to talk about what to do in Las Vegas as our food finally arrived.

While Matt and I ate, Maria got up and headed towards the front door. As she was walking by our area to leave, she took a long look at me with a smirk on her face. I kept my face toward my plate as if I was eating so Matt wouldn't notice me looking at her. I moved my eyes towards her with a blank stare. I did not know how to react to her looking at me like that. On the inside, however, I was getting more and more scared.

"Elizabeth, what are you looking at?" Matt said. My face turned red at the thought of him seeing me giving the stare, but I realized that as I was staring, I was holding a fork with food on it but not putting it in my mouth.

"Nothing," I said as I gave a nervous chuckle. "I'm curious. Matt. Is Maria in any way violent?"

"No. Maria would never hurt a soul."

"Does she get angry easily?"

"No."

"What does she do if she were angry at something? How does she express her anger?"

"If she gets angry, she says she needs to be alone. I don't know what she does when she is alone. Why are you curious about that stuff?"

I grew a little nervous after he asked that. I wondered what he would think of me when I told him I was starting to get scared of Maria, even though he told me not to worry. "Because

I saw Maria get mad at you at the diner this morning, and after she told you that you would regret it, it got me a little concerned, is all."

"I'm sure there's nothing to worry about. I'm sure Maria didn't mean to say that. Sometimes, when people are angry, they will say things they don't mean."

"True. So, do you have a favorite musician?"

We talked about music as we finished eating. Throughout our chat, I felt a knot in my stomach, mainly because I wondered what Matt thought of me after that conversation about Maria.

"Thanks for another wonderful dinner. Matt. It was pretty good," I said.

"No problem. You ready to go swimming?" Matt said.

"Don't we need to wait an hour after eating?"

"It's different for everyone. I know my stomach doesn't hurt when I go swimming after eating. Does yours?"

"I don't know. I've never swam right after eating before. But I guess there's only one way to find out."

The daycare workers always told me I could get a stomach ache if I swam right after eating, which made me scared to try it. However, I didn't want to wait forever to get into the pool with Matt, so I decided to try it.

Matt and I got into his jeep after Matt paid the bill. As Matt drove us to the apartments, I started thinking about Maria. I'm getting scared that she's up to something, and not knowing what it is, is driving me up the wall. Due to that, the ride back was silent for the most part, minus the radio playing.

"Come in! The water feels nice," Matt said after he jumped into the pool.

I started slowly stepping into the pool, thinking it would initially feel cold, even though Matt said it was lovely. After a few steps, I realized it was warm and walked in faster. After going underwater to get my hair wet, I watched Matt as he floated around.

"Doesn't this feel awesome?" Matt said once he returned to his feet a couple of minutes later.

"It sure does," I said. "Matt, I have to tell you something."

"What's up?" Matt started walking towards me.

"I know we've only known each other for a few days, but you're sweet, driven, and fun. I don't know about you, but I feel like we're a perfect match for each other. What do you think?"

"This is what I think about it," Matt said. Then he grabbed my shoulders and pulled me close to him. He put his lips against mine. I was not expecting that at all tonight. After he finished kissing me, I didn't know what to say except that I genuinely enjoyed the surprise.

"What do you think of that?" Matt said.

"I like it," I said.

Matt then smiled and then kissed me again. This time, it turned into a make out session. As we kissed, I wrapped my legs around his waist as he held me close. There were moments when I combed my fingers through his hair. I couldn't stop smiling from ear to ear when we finished kissing. I wish it didn't have to end. Like all first kisses, you want it to last forever.

Matt and I swam around the pool and played games briefly. We then sat in the jacuzzi for quite some time. While enjoying the relaxation of the jacuzzi. Matt and I kept talking and kissing each other a few times. Each time we kissed, I felt the spark between us. At one point, I even sat on his lap as we continued kissing each other. Now I know Matt is the one for me.

When Matt and I exited the jacuzzi, we dried ourselves off and told each other how much fun we had tonight.

After putting our clothes on over our swimsuits (after they were dry enough), Matt and I walked to the pool entrance door. I held the door open for Matt to go through first, and I followed behind him through that door. As he was walking in the hallway, I noticed a closet door was slightly cracked open. I thought that was weird because it was after business hours, but I figured maybe a night person was working, so I shook it off.

That was until, out of nowhere, a hand wearing a black glove and a long black sleeve came out of the closet with a knife. The person holding the knife remained hiding in the closet as they began to stab Matt outside of the closet.

The knife entered Matt's neck and then came out within a second. The knife then entered the side of Matt's chest as Matt was reaching for his neck wound. The knife came out of Matt's chest area, and Matt fell to the ground and landed on his knees at first. A couple of seconds later, Matt collapsed onto the floor landing on his belly with his head slightly turned to where his neck wound was almost facing upwards.

I screamed each time Matt got stabbed and as he collapsed onto the floor. I was shaking so hard that I wasn't sure I was able to hold my balance much longer. As I saw the closet door open slightly more at first, I dropped my towel while backing into the corner and tried my best not to breathe so hard to where the stabber could hear me. Fear was taking over my entire body, and tears started to shed. I thought this was the end of my life after it had just gotten perfect.

A second later, I see someone wearing black clothing and a black ski mask running towards the main entrance of the building. I was thankful that the person didn't see me, but I was disappointed that I didn't see the face. After not seeing the stabber in the area for more than a few seconds, I grabbed my towel and ran up to Matt as I saw him continuing to bleed very severely and gasping for air.

"T-t-t-t-o-o-wel," Matt said while he continued to gasp for air.

I got down on my knees and held my towel on his neck wound. While doing so, I noticed Matt's towel beside him and reached for it. I put that on Matt's chest wound and tried to hold it down with as much pressure as I could while continuing to hold my towel on his neck wound with my other hand.

"Stay with me. Matt!" I kept saying as Matt continually gasped for air.

I let go of his neck wound for a second but made sure the towel remained on the wound while I grabbed my cell phone out of my back pocket. After reaching it, I opened it up and dialed 911 immediately. As I put the phone between my shoulder and ear, I went back to putting pressure on Matt's neck wound.

Once the 911 operator answered, I reported the emergency.

CHAPTER 8

M att was strolled out of the complex on a gurney while I
spoke with the responding police officer. Tears kept streaming down my face like no tomorrow. I couldn't believe what had happened.

"We were just walking out of the pool entrance, and out of nowhere, someone stabbed Matt in the neck and chest area," I said.

"By any chance, did you get a glimpse of the person who did it?" the officer said.

"No. At first, I saw a hand wearing a black glove and a long black sleeve sticking out the door. When the person came out of the closet, I was in that corner and saw a thin-built person, maybe five-foot-twoish. I couldn't tell if it was a male or a female because that person wore all black and a black ski mask. The person didn't even look in my direction. That person just stepped out of the closet and ran for the exit."

"Do you know if Matt has any enemies?"

"I can't think of any enemies. I do know that his ex-girlfriend was mad that I started dating him. She kept trying to get back together with him. When he said 'no' to that, she angrily said, 'You will regret this one day'."

"Do you know the name of his ex?"

"Yes. It's Maria Frichmen."

"Okay. Anything else we need to know?"

"Not that I can think of at the moment."

"Here's the number to call if you have more information for us."

After the officer handed me a business card with the phone number on it, I started to walk away from the crime scene slowly, with more tears coming down my face. I looked at the crime scene one last time before leaving that area and heading to my apartment.

Once I reached my apartment, I threw on my pajamas and went to lay on my floor bed. As I lay on my right side, crying my eyes out, I couldn't stop repeating that event in my head. It was like watching a movie scene non-stop. It was nearly impossible to fall asleep because of that. I was constantly thinking of Matt and hoping he would recover from the stabbing. I kept crying and crying until I finally dozed off with a major headache that I got from all that crying.

The Bay City Police Station contacted me the following day and asked me to come to the police station for further questioning regarding Matt's stabbing. I notified Barbara at work that I couldn't go in and headed to the police station soon after.

While I was driving to the police station, I was listening to the local radio station. After hearing some advertisements, the radio show came back on.

"This is your host, the Great Gilbert, with you today. The news this morning is that a local EMT by the name of Matt Koniephe was killed last night at the Romando apartment complex," the radio said.

"What? No!" I said to myself as tears started filling my eyes.

"Police are still investigating the incident and have no suspect information."

"No! No! No!" I started smacking my steering wheel with one hand. I could hardly breathe as more and more tears filled my eyes. I couldn't believe what I heard. Matt died from the stabbing. I changed the radio station as I started to cry to see if there was music to help me focus on driving.

When I got to the police station, tears kept coming down, but I tried my best to stop, even though it was nearly impossible. I told the front desk why I was there, and the receptionist said she would notify the proper person that I had arrived.

While waiting, tears continued to come down my face. I kept trying to hide my face and wipe away tears so the people at the police station wouldn't see how I looked.

When I was a kid, Mom gave me many reasons to cry at home and in public places. Whenever I started to cry, Mom would smack me in the face and say things like, 'Stop being so stupid' or 'Nobody is going to like you being the constant crier you are' and more.

As I entered my teenage years, those past experiences made me try hard not to cry in front of Mom (at least) or other people. If I needed to cry, I would hold it until I was alone. Nowadays, I hold it in whenever I'm around people unless I cannot control it.

A police officer came out to the area I was waiting in and called me over to him. He escorted me to a room with a table, a clock, and chairs. As we sat down, he started asking questions about the incident.

"How long have you known Matt?" the officer asked.

I was nervous as the officer asked me the question. I've gone through a lot in my life, but nothing like this.

"A couple of days," I said, crossing my arms on the table before me and leaning my head forward.

"During the couple of days, did Matt say anything about having enemies?"

"No."

"Did you and Matt have any problems the past couple of days?"

"No problems. Although Matt's ex-girlfriend seemed to pop up wherever we went."

"Tell me more about that."

I explained everything I could to the officer about how Maria acted whenever I was with Matt.

After explaining that, the officer asked more questions until he got called to someone's office.

"I'll be right back, Elizabeth," he said.

As time ticked away, I mostly sat down and stared at the wall, tears in my eyes. There were also moments when I would have my head down on the table since I had nothing else to do but think about Matt and how he is now dead. And the thought that as things were becoming great with him and me, it's all gone since Matt died. The thought of that continuously ran through my head and brought more and more tears to my eyes.

When the officer came back in, he started asking more questions. He continued asking me questions about everything me and Matt did together, how Maria acted around me and Matt, and everything I saw and did when Matt got stabbed.

When the officer finished asking questions, he walked me to the main entrance and said they would call me if they had more questions.

My car was parked just across the street from the police station. It was against the curb on a two-way, two-lane road. I'm not one to park on the curb on busy streets because I'm always afraid someone will wreck my car. But in this case, that spot was the only spot I could find available close to the police station, so I had no choice but to face my fear. Thankfully, I could see my car was still in one piece.

The traffic light near the crosswalk showed the walk signal, and I started crossing the street on the crosswalk. A black car drove through the red light as I got halfway across. Noticing that the vehicle was not slowing down and was about to run into me, I immediately ran opposite from where I was walking. Thankfully, I returned to the sidewalk, where the police station was just in time.

I watched the black car go down a block from where I was and make a U-turn. The vehicle then returned to the light I was standing at and stopped at the light. I looked through the passenger window and noticed Maria was behind the wheel.

Wearing the same hat and trench coat she wore at the restaurant the night before; she pointed a finger at me and gave me an angry look. She mouthed toward me what looked like she was saying, 'You're next.' The traffic light then turned green, and Maria drove off.

My heart was racing as she drove away. What did Maria mean by saying that I was next exactly? The only thing I could think of when it comes to being 'next' is that I'll be the next one to get killed somehow, which raises another question. Was Maria the one who killed Matt? At the moment with the times I saw her following us, what she just said to me, and what she said to Matt at the diner, all signs were pointing to yes.

Once the signal changed, I walked on the crosswalk again, this time as fast as possible. When I reached the sidewalk on the other side of the street, I continued speed walking and watched my surroundings. Thankfully, I made it to my car safely.

As I got into my car and turned the ignition, I debated telling the police what just happened. I felt like I had to for my safety, but on the other hand, I wondered if I was losing my mind and maybe did not see what Maria meant to say even though she gave me an angry look. Ultimately, I decided to wait until I was certain Maria was doing something threatening to me. Although there is some evidence that she is up to something involving me, I want to be sure before I go as far as telling the police I don't feel safe because of her.

While driving home with the radio on, I tried to clear my head by thinking positively, which was impossible with everything going on. It was even more challenging to clear my head as I was driving through because whenever I saw a black car, I would get nervous and think it was Maria. One black car drove right behind me for most of the drive home. I grew increasingly anxious as the car made the same turns as I did. I kept trying to figure out who the person behind the wheel was but could not. That car eventually went in a different direction.

After I got to my apartment, I checked my mailbox and noticed I had some mail. Most of the mail were advertisements and other junk mail. I then saw an envelope with my name but no return address. Someone spelled my name with letter stickers, so there was no handwriting I could attempt to recognize. I was hesitant to open it, but I eventually opened it to see what it could be. That person also wrote the letter out in letter sticks and no handwriting.

TO: ELIZABETH
FROM: YOU DON'T NEED TO KNOW
SINCE I KNOW WHERE YOU LIVE, I WILL ONE DAY STOP BY AND WATCH YOU AS YOU TAKE YOUR FINAL BREATH.

My heart started racing. At that moment, I knew someone was out to kill me. And I had a gut feeling that it was Maria.

CHAPTER 9

Continuing to freak out, I went straight to Martha's apartment, hoping with all my heart that she was home. After seeing that letter, I was scared to be in my apartment, knowing that someone was out to kill me. And the fact that they knew where I lived scared me enough. I didn't know what I would do about it except maybe not be there for a while. Hopefully, Martha could help out with that.

Once I reached Martha's apartment, I knocked on her door. Within a few seconds, Martha opened the door. After she said I could come in, I started talking like crazy.

"Martha, I've got a serious problem! Someone is out to kill me!" I said as I started breathing heavily.

"Wait...kill you?! Why?" Martha said.

"I don't know why. I'm scared of staying in my apartment because this letter was in my mailbox."

I handed the letter to Martha. As she read it, her eyes widened.

"Oh my gosh! This sounds serious!" she said. "I think you better notify the police of this. You should also stay here just to be safe."

"I will go in the morning because I need to gather my thoughts after all these events that have been going on."

"Events?"

"Oh right, I haven't told you yet. Matt got stabbed during our date last night and died from his injuries," I started to feel tears forming in my eyes once again. I start rubbing my eyes as the tears start running down my face. "And Maria attempted to run me over with her car."

"Oh my goodness!" Martha took a deep breath and started showing a sad expression. "If Tim were here, I'm sure he would help protect you."

Sitting on Martha's couch next to her, I noticed tears forming in her eyes as I cried.

"Martha, what's wrong?" I said, trying to stop myself from crying more.

"Tim died in a car accident," Martha said, taking slow, deep breaths as she was about to start crying.

My eyes widened in shock. "Seriously?!"

Martha nodded her head and officially began crying.

"I saw the accident happen right in front of me as I was about to get into my car in the parking lot of your diner yesterday morning."

As I was still crying, Martha started explaining what she had seen. Martha said that as she was leaving the restaurant and heading to her car, she saw Jenny Harbor begin to pull out of the parking lot and get onto the main road. As Jenny started pulling out in her red Chevy Impala, Tim's black Nissan Altima T-boned her, likely because she didn't see him coming in the oncoming traffic, and it was too late for him to stop on time for Jenny to move out of the way. Seeing him go into the ambulance on the gurney, Martha got worried about his well-being. She ran to the paramedics and asked which hospital he was going to. When Martha got close to Tim, Martha saw a lot of blood on his head and face. After being informed where he was going, she immediately followed him to the hospital once emergency personnel cleared the road. Once she arrived at the emergency room, hospital staff informed Martha that Tim had passed away upon arrival at the hospital.

"Oh, Martha. Why do we both have to go through this?" I said as I hugged her, and she hugged me back. We cried on each other's shoulders until there was a knock at the door.

Martha attempted to wipe all her tears away, even though they kept forming. She looked through the peephole in her door and seemed to recognize who it was. After taking a deep breath and trying to collect herself, she opened the door, and a tall man with light brown hair and an average-sized man with blonde hair stood at the door.

"Tom. Brandon. What are you guys doing here?" Martha said, trying not to sound like she was crying.

"We didn't see you at work today, so we wanted to stop by and see if you were alright since you rarely miss work," the tall man named Tom said.

"You guys are sweet. I'm going through a loss right now. I'm sorry you have to see me like this."

"Don't worry. I still think you're beautiful."

Martha smiled slightly even though her tears were still running down her cheeks.

"Come on in, you guys."

The two guys walked in with Martha. I looked at her, confused, wondering who they were and why she was letting them in at a time like this.

"Elizabeth, this is Brandon and Tom. I work with them at the warehouse," Martha said.

"Nice to meet you," I said as I tried wiping my tears away.

Brandon sat down next to me and put his hand on my back. "Hey, what's the matter?"

"I'm going through a loss, too."

"I know what could help you relax."

"What's that?"

"A nice little walk through the park behind here. Walks always cheer me up."

"I doubt anything will cheer me up at this point."

"Come on. You'll enjoy it."

Brandon grabbed my hand and informed Martha and Tom that we would be back.

"I don't know if I feel safe going out there, Brandon," I said as we approached the door.

"You'll be safe with me. I promise."

We left the apartment and headed toward an area mostly covered with trees. I felt a little scared, but Martha didn't say anything bad about Brandon, so I figured I could feel safe around him.

As me and Brandon followed a walking path, we were getting to know each other. Eventually, our conversations helped me stop crying despite still feeling sad.

Brandon was a warehouse worker like Martha. The only difference is that he has his CDL license and drives a semi-truck for the company. When Brandon is not working, he hangs out with friends (Tom, for the most part) and goes fishing near his home. He and Tom have worked together for five years and are now considered each other's best friends.

Brandon and Tom met Martha when she first started working at the warehouse. Tom was training her, and he was smitten by her. Martha was not interested in Tom but enjoyed talking and hanging out with him and Brandon. With that, all three of them became close friends.

I explained to him my situation regarding someone looking to kill me and dealing with Matt's tragic death. Brandon reassured me that he would protect me whenever I felt the need to have protection. I thought that was sweet of him since we had just met.

"This is nice, Brandon," I said.

"I knew you would like it," he said. "Elizabeth, I have to ask you something."

"Yes, Brandon?"

I turned my head to look at Brandon. As I did, he gave me a smile you would see on a guy about to ask someone out on a date. He even took his thumb and brushed a strand of my hair out of my face. I honestly didn't know how to feel about it, seeing that I was still trying to get over Matt's death. On the other hand, how Brandon and I have been talking makes him seem very sweet. If he were to ask me out, I wouldn't want to hurt his feelings for the sweet guy he seems to be.

"You're friends with Rita Sanana, right? Do you have her number by any chance? I kind of have a crush on her," he said.

"Wait, what?" A part of me was relieved I didn't have to hurt his feelings by having to reject him, but the other part felt like he just tried to butter me up to get Rita's number. With that, I was sad and angry at the same time. I honestly felt used.

I just met this guy. He walked through the park with me and showed me a beautiful river view. Then he talked to me like he was about to ask me out and moved my hair out of my face—all that to ask for Rita's number. What gave him the idea that I was friends with Rita in the first place?

"You're friends with Rita Sanana, right?"

"No! Is that why you brought me here and said you would help protect me? So that you could get Rita's number?"

"No, of course not. I thought we could hang out and get your mind off everything."

"You think asking for Rita's number would get my mind off everything?"

"Elizabeth, you're taking this a little too far, don't you think?"

"Just leave Brandon! You don't know how to be a friend."

"Don't you want to come back to Martha's place?"

"I said LEAVE!" I pointed towards the walking path and gave him an angry stare until he finally started walking toward the path.

Brandon looked back at me a couple of times as he started walking away. As he walked away, I sat on the ground about a hundred feet away from the river. I was so upset and angry that I didn't want to deal with anyone. I wasn't even in the mood to speak to Martha.

I kept staring at the river as it was flowing.

I returned to Martha's apartment building. As I approached her apartment door, I overheard laughter.

"She acted like that indeed," Brandon laughed while I continued to listen to him, Tom, and Martha through the closed door.

"Ooh, I'm Elizabeth, and I'm scared of everything," I overheard Tom say while trying to impersonate me.

Everyone, including Martha, laughed at that. I certainly didn't like the guys talking and laughing about me, but hearing my best friend laugh with them kind of hurt. Martha would usually defend me if someone made fun of me, but it sounds like she is not this time.

"And she thought I was using her just to get Rita's number. That tells you how dumb she is."

After hearing Brandon say that, I got so mad I turned the doorknob and slammed the door open. Once it opened, I looked angry at everyone.

"Brandon, come here really quick. I have something to tell you," I said, speaking in a normal tone as if I wasn't angry while making a smirk towards him.

I grabbed his arm tightly as Brandon walked closer and pulled him outside the door.

"STAY OUT!" I yelled.

"What did you do that for?" Tom asked as he got up from his seat.

"Come here, and I'll tell you."

Once Tom walked up to me, I did the same thing to him. "AND STAY OUT!"

I then slammed the door shut on them. It felt good to express my anger toward them in that way.

Once I turned around, however, Martha looked at me with her hands on her hips, and I could tell she was mad.

"Elizabeth! What was that all about?" Martha said.

"You heard how they were making fun of me," I said. "Not to mention you were laughing too."

"Well, so you know, Tom and I are dating."

"But you just lost Tim the other day. Isn't it a little too soon to date again?"

"I don't see a problem with that."

"Whatever. That's still no excuse for letting those guys make fun of me."

"That may be true, but that doesn't mean you can throw them out the door like that."

"Why are you defending them making fun of me?"

"Tom was just trying to be funny."

"But it wasn't funny."

"Yes, it was. If you were here, you would've understood it better and thought it was funny."

"I understood enough that you laughed and didn't defend me after Tom impersonated me. Especially when Brandon went on to call me dumb."

Martha crossed her arms. "Well, I now agree with the dumb part."

'Is my best friend seriously talking to me like this?' was the only thing running through my mind. "Excuse me?"

"After what you just did, I agree you are dumb."

"I can't believe you!" I started walking toward the door, seeing the conversation going nowhere.

"Just know, Elizabeth, once you walk out that door, we are no longer friends."

"Why? Do I have to accept that your boyfriend makes fun of me?"

"We're no longer friends because you obviously can't accept me and Tom as a couple. And I'd rather have a friend that does."

"Well, I'd rather have a friend that defends me when I'm being made fun of by her boyfriend."

I walked out the door and slammed it shut behind me. Brandon and Tom were still standing outside Martha's door, watching me as I started to walk toward my apartment building. As scared as I was to return to my apartment, it seemed like I had no choice but to try to go there, especially now that I have no friends. Martha was not only my best friend but my only friend for the most part. Now I have nobody.

I looked back towards Martha's apartment as I continued walking away. I saw Brandon and Tom get let back into Martha's apartment. I shook my head and continued walking.

Why would my best friend of ten years choose two guys over me? I was very sad and angry at the same time. I don't think I'll be able to forgive her for that. Never.

Once I got there, I walked into my apartment and went to turn on the lights. When I hit the light switch, the lights did not come on. I knew my electric bill was nowhere near due because I had just moved here and activated it a few days ago. I figured a fuse blew or something.

"Hello, Elizabeth," said a woman's voice.

As I turned my head to see who said that, I saw nothing but a closed fist coming towards my face. Before I knew it, I felt a big punch in my face. As I fell to the ground from the force of that punch, everything turned utterly black.

CHAPTER 10

I opened my eyes and found myself in an empty room while being tied up to a stair rail. My wrists were tied together with one end of the rope while the other end was tied to the railing above my head as I sat on a cold, hard floor. My mouth was covered with duct tape as well. Aside from the railing, the only other things in this area were a light bulb hanging from the ceiling and a stairway towards my left. The area did not look familiar to me. I couldn't recall ever seeing this area.

While trying to comprehend where I was, I saw a shadow slowly descending the stairs.

"Nice to see you're awake, Elizabeth," said the unknown voice.

Once she got down the stairs, I immediately recognized her. She came up to me and quickly took the duct tape off my mouth.

"Tiffany?" I said.

After I said that, she grabbed her hair at the base of her forehead and pulled it behind her head, revealing she was wearing a wig. She then removed her contact glasses.

"Rita?! Why are you doing this to me?" I said as my eyes widened in fear.

Rita gave an evil smile. "Oh, Elizabeth. There's no need to be afraid. It's just like the fun times we had in high school, where I was the best of the best, and you were the worst of the worst."

"And what does that have to do with this?"

"I saw your life going in the right direction for once, and I cannot allow that to happen. You get a place of your own, find a potential boyfriend, and enjoy your day-to-day life. There's no way I'll allow that. You do not deserve a better life. I deserve a better life."

Rita slapped me across the face with her hand. I slowly started to shed tears because of the sharp pain I was feeling from it. However, I tried my best to hold back the crying because I wanted her to see that I could be strong.

"How is my life better than yours? My life is falling apart if you ask me," I said.

"I enjoyed seeing how hard life was for you in high school, dealing with your mom and such. But once I read about your mom burning down your house in the newspaper and got told by Linda that you moved into one of her apartments, I thought things were going to get better for you. I certainly don't want to see that happen," Rita said.

"So, are you the one that sent me that threatening letter?"

Rita smiled as if satisfied with how her plan succeeded, "Yes."

"Are you going to leave me here to die then?"

"Oh yes," Rita returned the duct tape to my mouth. "I'll return at some point because I can't afford to miss out on seeing you slowly die."

I kept trying to untie my wrists. After struggling for quite some time, I gave up. I even took my shoes and socks off by foot and tried to pull the rope apart with my toes, but that was unsuccessful.

For the most part, I could only watch the light bulb swing back and forth whenever a little air was blown down to here.

While staring at the light bulb or the walls around me, I kept thinking about what Rita would do to kill me. I imagined how she would attack me with a baseball bat, a shovel, or some blunt object. I even imagined her shooting me with a gun.

Aside from imagining those things, I was also thinking about my life. I was thinking about what I went through as a kid, as a teenager, and as an adult. I couldn't think of too many positive things about my life. All I could think of were my good times, such as high school graduation, getting my first car, and getting my apartment. It seemed like I was having a positive change in my life for once. And as soon as it became positive, it's likely to end sooner than I thought.

Sometimes, I would close my eyes and sleep in the one position I was in. It wasn't the most comfortable position, but it had to do since I could hardly move.

Occasionally, I would attempt to make some noise. I tried screaming for help even though my mouth was covered with duct tape. There was no luck with that, though.

It was unclear to me how long I'd been down here. There was no clock anywhere, and I didn't have my phone. It already felt like hours had passed, but I was unsure if it had even been an hour.

My stomach started growling, and my mouth was craving meat. As I was thinking about meat, Rita came down the stairs with a brown paper bag.

Rita took the duct tape off my mouth and sat against the wall across from me. Rita then put her hand into the bag and took out a cheeseburger.

"You must be hungry. Would you like half of this cheeseburger?" Rita said as she unwrapped the cheeseburger from the wrapper.

"Sure," I said, hoping I could at least have a bite. My mouth was watering just seeing that cheeseburger. I wanted a bite of it so badly that I would do anything.

"Well, too bad!" Rita took a bite of the burger. "You don't deserve it."

I just sat back and smirked at Rita, thinking it was worth a shot. I didn't have my hopes too high, seeing that Rita was trying to kill me.

Every time she took a bite of the burger, I couldn't help but feel a big craving for it. I made a look of jealousy toward Rita while she continued eating.

"That's right, Elizabeth. I'm enjoying every single bit of this," Rita said.

"And why do I care about that?" I said.

"Because I can imagine how hungry you are right now. I'm sure seeing this makes you miserable, which is what I'm enjoying."

I kept giving Rita a blank stare because I had nothing to say.

"You know how I've always gotten what I wanted in high school? Well, I'm making sure I keep getting what I want. The last thing I want is someone I know to have it better than me.

"I was on top of the world after high school. I was the head cheerleader at the local university, dating the hot quarterback, working as a makeup artist and founder of my makeup studio, and getting my education in fashion design. I lost all of that after I got into a serious car accident. I got seriously injured, and I could not cheer anymore. Thanks to that, I lost my scholarship and couldn't afford school. I had to close my makeup studio because I wasn't making enough to keep it going.

"Just when I thought things couldn't get worse in my life, it did. My boyfriend decided to cheat on me with the new head cheerleader.

"Now here I am, stuck working as a stinking housekeeper!"

I was shocked when Rita told me how her life turned upside down after high school. I always thought she would have it made in the adult world, but I guess, like most people, she faced some hardships.

"If you don't like it, why did you apply?" I asked.

"Because stupid, I needed the money as soon as possible. With that, I had no choice but to apply to any place that was hiring. Even if I didn't like it!" Rita took another bite of her cheeseburger. "And that's why I'll keep you here until you take your final breath. It'll make my downhill life seem better."

Rita kept talking to me while she continued eating her food. She went on about her unsuccessful life as if I was her therapist. I didn't understand why she was telling me all that stuff. It seemed, however, that if I made it seem like I was listening to her, I had less chance of getting hurt by her.

Rita started mentioning how her sister was the most successful of the two. Rita was jealous of Linda.

Growing up in a wealthy family, Rita was the spoiled brat, and Linda was the over-achiever. Rita got whatever she asked her parents for. If she wanted a new car just because she didn't like the one she had, her parents got it for her without hesitation. Rita always had expensive brand clothes, makeup, handbags, and other things every teenager wanted. She was hoping that one day she would have her own brand of fashion, which was why she went into fashion design in college. While in college, she thought about getting a head start with her career by owning a makeup studio that would eventually sell her fashion brand along with doing makeup.

After Rita's serious car accident, she was out of work and school for quite some time. When she could work again, the business wasn't making enough income to continue, which forced her to sell it. The money received from selling the company was given to her parents since they were the ones who purchased it for her.

Rita asked her parents if they could help her return to college since she lost her scholarship. But her parents said no because they already made a big purchase for her. They felt it would be unfair to Linda if they made a second big purchase for Rita when they haven't for Linda.

Their parents spoiled Linda while growing up, but she didn't have an expensive taste like Rita. Whatever their parents gave to Linda, she was happy with it. She went to college on a scholarship after receiving a high-grade point average. Linda got her Bachelor's and Master's degrees in Business Administration. While in college, she worked at a local clothing store with five locations around the Bay City area. After working there for a few years, Linda got promotion after promotion. She eventually became vice president of the company.

A couple of years later, Linda noticed the Romando Apartment complex was for sale by its owner. She saw it as a great investment opportunity and believed she could make money on the side while still working as vice president of the clothing company.

Linda brought the idea up to her parents, who assisted her in fully buying the property. They paid for the apartment entirely under one condition: Her parents were cutting her off financially except for emergencies, and she couldn't ask for any more purchases. This condition was the same as they gave Rita when they bought her the makeup studio.

Linda was not too worried about her parents cutting her off. She knew she could care for herself financially and knew the investment and hard work would pay off in no time. While the hard work paid off for Linda, it didn't pay off for Rita, which upset her.

"Is that why you kidnapped me? To tell me your sob story?" I said.

"No, you stupid idiot! I already told you. I get amused by your life going downhill. Or, in this case, watch your life slowly end," Rita said.

"Then why tell me your sob story then?"

"Because moron, it'll make time go a little quicker since it can be quite a long journey before your final breath. And, of course, sitting and watching you while you're alive is not fun enough."

"Well, to kill time, why don't you visit Brandon at Martha's place?"

"Who is Brandon?"

"A guy who has a crush on you. He used me to get your phone number and then made fun of me. And thanks to him, I lost my best friend."

"Hmm...It sounds like he might have the same point of view on you, just like I do. I shall go visit him and see." Rita slapped my face again and kept her face close to mine, "I'll be right back, you idiot."

I was expecting her to put the duct tape back on my mouth, but shockingly, she didn't. I wasn't sure if she happened to forget or figured I was getting weak enough not to scream for help. Better yet, she probably thought it was getting late enough that nobody would walk around in the area I was in.

CHAPTER 11

I slept for quite some time—at least, it felt like it. There were times I was hoping to die in my sleep so I wouldn't have to deal with being stuck here waiting for something good or bad to happen. I was tired of feeling so hungry. I was tired of looking at nothing but a light bulb swinging back and forth at times. I was even tired of trying to make noise to get help while Rita was gone. I also got tired of the emotional and physical pain I was experiencing from this. Last but not least, I was tired of sitting in one position.

At one point, with my eyes closed, I felt something wet and slimy rub against my cheek. I thought I was dreaming as I heard what sounded like heavy breathing. Before I knew it, I felt the slimy touch on my cheek again. I slowly opened my eyes and found a Siberian Husky standing beside me. Seeing the dog, the first thing I thought would happen was that the husky would end up mauling me to death. With that, I was shaking a little bit in fear.

The dog kept licking me here and there, and as it kept licking me, I would slowly get less scared. Especially since after every lick, he would stand there and stare at me with his tongue sticking out in a smiling way.

It felt gross having the husky's tongue against my face, but at the same time, I would prefer that over him trying to eat me. Seeing that the dog wasn't mauling me, at least not right away, I figured this dog could help me forget about my fears and would keep me company until Rita came back.

I kept talking to the dog to kill the time. The dog would stand by and occasionally sit with his tongue out as if he were listening to me. At times, he would continue licking my face here and there to respond to me.

As I continued talking to him, I felt like I had to give him a name. Eventually, I started calling him Lucky. I decided Lucky would be a good name for him because I was lucky to have him with me for some company during this rough, slow, torturous time.

"Hey Lucky, can you roll over?" I said.

In response, Lucky rolled over.

"Can you sit?"

Lucky sat down.

"You seem to be well trained. If only you could talk."

Lucky licked my face again.

I looked down at the floor. "The other question is, are you someone's dog?"

As I imagined what it would be like to have Lucky as a dog, I heard Lucky growling. I looked at him to see what he was doing, and it appeared he was chewing on the rope attached to the railing. I figured he was playing with it. The rope eventually detached from the railing. I brought my arms down to my lap.

"Lucky! You freed me from the railing! You're such a good dog!" I said.

I looked at the rope around my wrists, then Lucky, then my wrists again, and then Lucky again.

"Lucky, can you get the rope off my wrists too?" I said as I put my hands near Lucky's mouth.

Lucky bit the rope around my wrists and was able to loosen it. Once it was loose enough, I could take the rope off my wrists. I immediately hugged Lucky. Since Lucky freed me, I wanted to keep him as a pet. There was no collar around his neck or contact information anywhere. I hoped nobody owned him so he could be my dog.

"You're such a good boy! At least I think you're a boy," I said as I scratched his chin.

Realizing I had to get out of the area quickly before Rita came back, I tied the rope that had me tied up and tied it around Lucky's neck so I wouldn't lose him while I was trying to get away from Rita.

After I put on my socks and shoes, Lucky and I started walking up the stairs. We walked up the stairs slowly to ensure Rita wouldn't pop up out of nowhere. When we reached the top of the stairs, I saw a sign on my right that said 'Tornado Shelter' with an arrow pointing toward the stairs.

I took a few steps forward, hoping to recognize where I was exactly. When I reached an outdoor lamp, I realized we were still at the Romando apartments.

Feeling relieved, I started fast walking with Lucky's help to return to my apartment. However, I was weak enough to where I could only fast walk so much. Lucky got ahead of me far enough that the rope would stretch while I held onto it. He would walk at a good pace to keep me going. I felt so hungry and sore in places to where I wasn't sure I could walk anymore. If Lucky had not been with me, I probably would have fallen by now and would have been unable to get up. I probably wouldn't be motivated to get up until someone found me. That is if they ever found me.

"Elizabeth!" I heard come from behind me.

I stopped in my tracks and got Lucky to stop. My eyes widened, and I turned to see if I was just hearing things. It turned out Rita was standing about ten feet away from us. She started to stroll towards us.

"I was hoping I didn't have to go this far. But now you leave me with no choice," Rita growled as she reached into her pocket.

Once she got her hand out of her pocket, I noticed what looked like a kitchen cutting knife in her hand.

"I tried to kill you once, but now I'm going to kill you for sure. Only this time, I won't stab the wrong person," Rita said as she pointed the knife towards me and continued strolling towards us.

"You mean you killed Matt?" I said as I started to walk backwards slowly.

"Yes, I did. But really, I meant to kill you."

"Then why did you kill Matt?"

"As I saw you two walking out of the pool entrance, I thought you would be ahead of him. So, I took my chance and stabbed what I thought was you. Unfortunately, I was wrong. Now, this time, I will succeed."

"Lucky, run!" I told Lucky, hoping he would get a head start on running.

Lucky immediately started running, and I ran behind him. Rita started running after us not long afterward. After a few moments of running, I was beginning to grow weaker, to the point where I felt I was about to fall and not get up. However, as Lucky and I were almost at the walking trail behind the complex, Lucky picked up speed a little bit and got me running faster, forcing me to fight the pain and weakness I was experiencing.

As we continued running, I kept looking behind me every few seconds to ensure Rita wasn't getting closer. At one point, when I was looking behind me, I ran into a tree and fell to the ground. I also ended up letting go of the rope. At that point, I was unable to move, thanks to the pain I endured from hitting that tree and falling. I also felt fragile, knowing it wasn't worth getting up. In my mind, all I could think was that it was time for it to end. I closed my eyes and waited for Rita to stab me to death.

I wasn't ready to die—especially this young. But I knew I could not save myself at this point unless a miracle happened.

Suddenly, I hear Lucky barking and growling. I also heard what seemed like Rita screaming. The screaming and barking got quieter by the second.

"OW! YOU STUPID DOG!" I heard Rita yell at one point.

I wanted to see what was happening but felt too weak to open my eyes as I remained on the ground, waiting for Rita to end my life. Eventually, I fell into a deep sleep.

"Can you explain to me how you found her?" I heard a male voice say.

"I was sitting in my tent reading a book when I heard someone screaming. I exited my tent and found her lying on the ground a few feet away. I attempted to wake her up by tapping her a few times, but she wasn't responding. That's when I called 911," a woman's voice said.

I opened my eyes slowly and found myself lying in a bed with machines beeping next to me. At first, I thought I was dreaming. I closed my eyes and shook my head to get myself out of that dream, but I was still in the same place when I opened my eyes again.

A young woman with long, straight, light brown hair and a police officer were sitting in the chairs next to the bed I was lying on.

"Where am I?" I said as I was moaning.

"Hello, I'm Officer Phillips from the Bay City Police Department. You're in the hospital right now being treated for some injuries," Officer Phillips said.

"Did I get stabbed?"

"No. You fell pretty hard."

I was relieved to hear that Rita didn't stab me.

"Is this your dog by any chance?" Officer Phillips said while holding onto the rope still attached to Lucky.

"Lucky!" I reached over the side of the hospital bed and started petting Lucky, "He's been with me since he rescued me. He seemed to be a stray dog or something, so I'm not sure if he belongs to anyone."

"What do you mean rescue you?"

I told the officer the story of everything Rita did to me. I explained all she did while keeping me tied up in the tornado shelter and what she admitted to me after I escaped. The officer took notes on what I was saying. After completing his notes, he told me he would call me if he needed more information.

As the officer left the room, the woman with him remained in her seat and stared at me. I stared back at her for a second, confused because I didn't recognize her.

"Hi, I'm Hannah Donald. I found you near my tent in the park and called the ambulance," she said.

"Thank you very much for saving me, Hannah. I'm Elizabeth Monter. I have to pay you back somehow," I said.

"Don't worry about it. I'm just glad to see you're okay."

"Did you witness anything happen before you called the ambulance?"

"I did see a girl running as your dog was barking and chasing her. I'm guessing he bit her because, at some point, I heard her yell, 'Ow. You stupid dog.' After that, he returned to you and sat beside you."

"Lucky saved me again?" Tears formed in my eyes because I never thought a dog could be a lifesaver. It made me want to keep him as a pet even more. I petted Lucky more, and he licked my face a few times. "Lucky, I wouldn't be alive now if it wasn't for you. I love you, Lucky!" Lucky licked my face again.

"You're lucky to have Lucky."

I chuckled at how she matched Lucky's name to me being lucky. "I know. I wish I could find out if he has an owner."

I told Hannah she didn't have to stay if she didn't want to, but she insisted on staying. I thought that was nice of her, seeing that we just met.

Hannah and I got to know each other a little bit. She works as an administrative assistant at a car dealership. Aside from camping, Hannah likes baking, reading, and anything to do with nature. She offered me cookies she made and had with her for her camping trip. Because I was still starving, I immediately accepted her offer.

I ate the cookies she gave me very quickly. They were your typical chocolate chip cookies, but they tasted fantastic.

Hannah is a couple of years older than me. She also lives at the Romando apartments, but she lives a building down from mine.

After Hannah finished telling me about herself, I started telling her about my life with my mom and how my life has been living there.

After I finished telling her those stories, Hannah put her hand on my arm.

"I'm sorry you had to go through all that, Elizabeth. Just know that I will always be here for you," Hannah said.

"Thanks, Hannah. You are very nice," I said.

There was a knock at the door. The door then opens, and the doctor walks in.

"Miss Elizabeth, how are you feeling?" the doctor said.

"I'm okay. Still sore," I said.

"Good news is your X-rays don't show anything wrong. Likely, you're just experiencing bruising. I suggest you take some ibuprofen to reduce the pain. Do you have any questions for me?"

"How long am I staying?"

"I'm going to get your discharge papers now, and you should be good to go."

CHAPTER 12

Hannah took Lucky and me to her one-bedroom apartment. The walls had many nature photos, and plants grew on the window sill.

"I can tell you enjoy nature," I said as I looked around.

"Oh yes. It's probably my number one passion," Hannah said.

"What got you into it?"

"I always walked down a trail near my house when I was younger. Every time I walked down it, I found something fascinating. Sometimes, I would sit and stare at something nature-related."

"That's interesting. I always enjoy watching the river flow."

"Yeah. Those are nice. You and I should go on nature walks. Wouldn't that be fun?"

"It would be fun."

"Cool! Let's exchange numbers, and I'll text you when I'm up for a walk."

"You know what, I bet my phone is at my apartment. Let me give you my number, and you can text me saying it's you."

I put my phone number into Hannah's phone and thanked her again for her help.

Afterward, Lucky and I left her apartment and started walking toward mine. I was excited to get home after all the madness finally. Although my apartment was the place where Rita kidnapped me, I wanted to be back in my place and have my space. Was I scared Rita would come back for me? Yes, I was. But I would have to take extra precautions to protect myself. And I certainly did not want to ask Hannah for any favor after she saved my life.

Hannah seemed like a nice person. I may have found a new close friend to take over Martha's place.

When I got to my apartment, I realized I didn't have my keys. Hoping for good luck, I turned the doorknob, and the door opened. Then I found my keys and phone sitting on the floor. I was a bit shocked Rita didn't take them with her after the kidnapping to try to keep me from getting help or from getting home.

I immediately grabbed my phone and saw that Hannah had texted me. I began the process of saving Hannah's number.

"Don't think you're getting away this time, Elizabeth," I heard.

My eyes widened as I turned to find Rita holding the kitchen knife. This time, she was wearing a bandage on her leg, which was likely where Lucky bit her earlier.

Lucky started growling at Rita. As he did, Rita then grabbed a dog bone out of her pocket and showed it to Lucky. After Lucky saw the bone, he stopped growling and had his tongue sticking out of his mouth, showing Rita that he would like the bone. Rita threw the bone behind her, and Lucky went after it. Once Lucky got it, a cage door closed behind him, trapping him in a dog cage.

I started shaking as I tried to continue to save Hannah's number so I could call for help. Rita, however, slapped the phone out of my hand. After she did that, my phone landed in front of Lucky's cage. The phone remained flipped open after it landed in front of the dog cage, and Lucky stuck his paw through a hole in the cage door and started playing with my phone.

Rita got closer to me and was pointing the knife at me. I slowly backed up until I reached the wall.

"I'm done playing games. It's time for you to go, Elizabeth," Rita said. "Say goodbye, loser!"

"Rita, let's talk about this," I said as I became increasingly frightened. "I'm sure there's a better way to settle this."

"There is no better way to settle this! No one I know should have a better life than me. And I'm going to make sure of it."

"But you always got what you wanted, and I never got anything but an alcoholic mother."

"That was before when my life was better than yours. Now, I need to make my life better again. And the only way to do that is by getting rid of you!"

"But this will not make your life better. This isn't the way to go about it."

"Yes, it is! Now shut up, and let me finish this!"

At that point, I felt there was no way to convince her not to do what she was about to do. I first looked from side to side, seeing if there was a way that I could run. After taking a few seconds to devise a plan to escape, I started running, but Rita grabbed my arm to where I couldn't break free. Rita then pulled me close and pushed me toward the wall. As I was facing the wall, the palms of my hands were on the wall. Rita kept her hand against my back and put enough force to keep me pushed toward the wall so I wouldn't attempt to escape.

"Rita, please! Don't do this!" I pleaded.

"Shut up!" Rita said.

My life flashed through my mind. I thought of memories from my childhood and high school years, as well as the recent memories. Tears started running down my cheeks. I didn't want my life to end this soon, not this way.

Before I knew it, I felt a sharp pain in my back. As I screamed in pain, I felt the knife stab me a second time. I slowly slid down against the wall and then fell to the floor. First, I landed on my knees and eventually lay on my back. I opened my eyes briefly and saw that my sight was slowly fading. I started gasping for air.

Next, I heard a loud noise, as if someone had forced their way into the apartment.

"Put your hands up where I can see them!" I heard.

I wanted to see if what I heard was happening, but I couldn't move a muscle—I couldn't even move my neck.

As I stared at the ceiling, my vision got more and more blurred by the second. As seconds passed, I was having more trouble breathing.

Eventually, I stopped breathing, and my vision was completely gone.

CHAPTER 13

"Rita Sanana was arrested at the scene where the crime took place. Rita remains in Bay City jail without bond," said the Bay City police chief at a press conference. As cameras were flashing, he continued with the timeline of events.

"Rita was hiding in the victim's apartment, waiting for the victim to arrive home. Once the victim arrived, Rita punched the victim in the face and knocked her unconscious. Rita then dragged the victim to the apartment's tornado shelter, tied her to a stair railing, and duct-taped her mouth closed. The victim was left down there alone for roughly ten hours without food or water. Occasionally, Rita went down to the shelter and spoke to the victim. There were times that she also slapped the victim in the face.

"At one point, a stray dog appeared in the tornado shelter where the victim was and freed the victim from the railing. Once the victim was free, she took the dog and tried to get to her apartment. Rita then found the victim before she could get home and went after the victim with a kitchen knife. The victim ran to a nearby trail and accidentally ran into a tree, which knocked her unconscious. As Rita was about to stab the victim, the dog chased Rita away and bit Rita's leg a couple of times. Eventually, the dog returned to the victim once Rita was gone.

"While the dog was chasing Rita away, a woman camping in the area found the victim unconscious and called for help. That woman remained with the victim at the hospital.

"After getting discharged from the hospital, the victim headed home. Rita happened to be in her home once again. Rita trapped the dog in a cage so it didn't chase her away or bite her again. The victim attempted to call for help, but Rita slapped the phone out of the victim's hand before she could call for help.

"The victim's phone landed in front of the dog cage. The dog was able to put his paw through a hole in the cage door and press a few buttons on the phone. After the dog pushed a few buttons, the phone called the woman who saved the victim earlier. The woman overheard what was going on and called the police.

"When the police arrived, they found the victim lying on the floor in a pool of blood. She was unresponsive and was taken to the Bay City hospital immediately while police took Rita in custody."

"This must be hard for you to watch this," Hannah said while watching the television.

"No. Rita has always been out to get me since high school, and now karma bit her in the ass for going too far," I said while lying down on a hospital bed, petting Lucky's head as he laid his head near me. "I just wish karma bit her sooner before all this happened."

"Isn't this going to haunt you the rest of your life?"

"It possibly could, but I'll probably have to learn to live with it."

Upon arrival at the hospital, I was taken into emergency surgery, went through a blood transfusion, and then got stitches in my back, where I got stabbed. I woke up about forty-eight hours later. When I woke up, the doctors told me that it was a miracle that I was still alive after what happened. They also said I would likely stay in the hospital for about a week to ensure that the stab wounds recovered thoroughly enough to get on with life. Aside from the stabbing, there were bruises around my nose and cheek area from where Rita punched me in the face before she kidnapped me. In my opinion, I looked like a monster.

"You know, I just realized something," I said. "My apartment will likely be a crime scene for some time. Where am I going to stay until then?"

"You could always stay with me," Hannah said.

"Hannah, I don't want to invade your space. Especially after all you've done for me."

"Don't worry. I've got your back, Elizabeth. Stay at my place as long as you need to."

"Thank you, Hannah. I have to repay you somehow."

"Again, don't worry about it."

I smiled at Hannah. I couldn't believe a woman could be this nice to me after all I've been through. What did I do to deserve her besides losing my best friend? I don't know how I would have gone on or even survived this situation and the attack I went through.

A nurse entered my room wearing a face mask, surgical scrub hat, and scrubs.

"Miss Elizabeth, the doctor told me to give you your discharge papers. I need you to sign here and here," the nurse said while pointing to where I had to sign.

Hannah and I looked at each other, confused. "The doctor just told us I would likely be here for a week," I said.

"Well, he just informed me that you are getting discharged. He said everything appears to be healing correctly and advised that you try to relax and not lift heavy items."

"Uh...okay?"

Something did not feel right about the nurse's words, but I signed the paperwork, and the nurse left the room.

"That was weird," Hannah said.

"I know. How does that happen? First, I get told I'll be in the hospital for about a week and then get told to go home."

"I don't know. Let's get you home, and I'll take care of you when I'm not working."

I lay on the couch at Hannah's apartment while Lucky sat on the floor next to the sofa. I couldn't stop wondering what the hell that hospital discharge was all about. I was sure I would be there for at least a week or month. Granted, I didn't feel too bad to go on with my life, but I would feel a small amount of pain in my back here and there, depending on how I moved.

The only thing I knew for sure was I had to be careful while my back continued to heal.

Unfortunately, that meant I would have to stay off work for some time. As soon as I realized that, I contacted Barbara and informed her I would be unavailable for work for at least a week. Barbara responded understandingly but said I would need a doctor's note so it couldn't be held against me.

After getting off the phone with Barbara, I called the hospital to ask for a return-to-work note.

"We will mail that note to you as soon as possible," the nurse said over the phone.

"Okay. Can my friend pick it up by any chance?" I said.

"Only you can come pick up the letter, but because of your injuries, we advise that you stay home and rest while we mail it to you. So, I'm sorry."

I rolled my eyes, annoyed that I had to do it the hard way. "Okay. Thank you."

After getting off the phone with the hospital, I stared at the ceiling while lying down on the couch in the best way I could without feeling pain. As I did, Hannah came to the living room area and sat in her chair with a cup of tea.

"Something happened?" Hannah said.

"I got told I need a doctor's note to excuse my absence from work. When I called the hospital, they said they would have to mail it and can't allow you to pick it up."

"Ouch."

"Tell me about it."

"On the bright side, you don't have to worry about Rita coming after you now that she is in jail."

"That's for sure. Thank goodness for that."

As Hannah sipped on her tea, her phone rang. She checked the caller ID, which appeared important because her eyes widened, and she quickly put down her tea to pick up the phone.

"Hello?" Hannah answered. "What? How? I'll be right there!"

Hannah got off the phone and immediately grabbed her purse. She told me that something important had come up about work and that she had to take care of it as soon as possible. I didn't even get to say a word because once she told me she had to leave, she quickly left Lucky and me at her place alone.

As I lay down on the couch and petted Lucky, I debated what to do while I rested. Part of me wanted to read Hannah's nature magazines or watch TV, but the other part just wanted to sleep.

I closed my eyes briefly and relaxed when I suddenly heard the door open. When I opened my eyes, I was expecting to see Hannah walking back in, but the person I saw was Martha. I slowly got up into the sitting position.

"Martha, what are you doing here?" I asked, looking at her confused and angry.

"Elizabeth, I'm sorry," Martha said.

"For what?"

"I'm sorry for laughing with the boys and defending them when they made fun of you."

"Thanks," I wasn't sure I could forgive her for what happened. "How did you know I was staying here?"

"I saw you walking in here as I pulled into the parking lot. I'm glad you're okay after what Rita did to you."

"Thanks."

"After I saw the story on the news, I felt so terrible for what I did to you. Can you please forgive me?"

I went silent. I did not know how to feel or what to think about that. I wanted to believe Martha because she had been my best friend forever. Yet after what happened the other day, I didn't know if I could forgive her for choosing a boy who makes fun of her best friend over her best friend. As a firm believer in forgiveness, I felt she deserved a second chance.

"Sure, I forgive you."

Martha carefully hugged me.

"Thanks, Elizabeth. I'll do whatever it takes to make it up to you. Who is your friend here?"

"This is Lucky. He saved my life."

"He is such a cutie!"

Lucky walked up to Martha so she could pet him. Martha rubbed his chin while he stood there.

"Yeah. When Rita tied me up in the tornado shelter, Lucky eventually came down and bit the rope to where it got untied. He also saved me by chasing Rita away when she was chasing after me with a knife."

"Dang. That sounds scary!"

"Oh, it was. If Lucky hadn't been around, I probably would have died."

"Is that why you call him Lucky? Because you were lucky to have him?" Martha chuckled.

"Yeah, pretty much," I chuckled also.

"I must go. But I'll talk to you soon, okay? And hopefully, you will be in your apartment again soon."

"Okay. See you later, Martha. I'm glad we're friends again!"

"Me too!"

Martha walked out the door, and I slowly laid back down. Not long after I laid back down, I closed my eyes. Then, the door opens again, and I quickly open my eyes.

"Well, that was weird. I get told by a coworker that I haven't submitted the paperwork that the boss requested. She told me she would wait for me there, but the doors were locked when I got to work. I knocked on the doors, and nobody was there," Hannah said as she threw her purse onto the floor and returned to her chair.

"Maybe that coworker realized that the paperwork wasn't needed immediately and decided to leave the place?" I said.

"I doubt it. I'm sure the coworker would have called back and said so. Especially since I said that I would be right there."

"I guess. Is your work nearby? Because you just left about five minutes ago."

"Yeah. It's only a few blocks down the main street."

"That's convenient."

"Yeah. Are you doing okay?"

"Yeah. I got a surprise visit from Martha."

"Who?"

"Oh, right. I probably haven't told you about my friendship with Martha."

I explained to Hannah how Martha and I have been best friends for a long time. I even explained to her the most recent events that almost destroyed our friendship for good. Hannah was a bit shocked when I discussed the most recent event. She shook her head in astonishment while opening her mouth slightly.

"What kind of best friend would do such a thing?" Hannah said.

"My best friend, I guess."

"She doesn't deserve to be a friend if she chooses a man over a best friend. Shows you what kind of person she is."

"Tell me about it. The weird thing was how Martha came over here while you were gone and apologized to me."

"She apologized? How did she know you were here?"

"She happened to see me walk into your apartment."

"Oh. I would be careful with her. If she acted like that once, there is no telling how she will act this time."

"I will. I just feel like after being close friends for so long, she deserves a second chance."

"Do what you feel is right. But Just be careful."

As Hannah and I watched TV, my phone started ringing.

"Hello?" I answered.

"Hey, Elizabeth!" Martha said.

"Hey, Martha. What's up?"

"Want to have dinner at my place?"

"Sure. When?"

"In about thirty minutes?"

"Okay. Can Hannah come too?"

"Maybe another time. I want tonight to be just you and me to make up for my actions."

"Okay. I'll be there soon."

I hung up the phone, and Hannah looked at me with a questioning look.

"Martha wants me to have dinner at her place tonight," I said.

"Oh. What did she say about me coming?" Hannah said.

"Martha wants tonight to be just me and her. She says next time she will invite you, though."

"Okay. You going to need help getting there?"

"Yeah, probably. Can you drive me there? Even though it's a couple of buildings down, I don't want to walk too much while my back is healing."

"Sure."

CHAPTER 14

Hannah dropped me off in front of Martha's apartment building, and I slowly walked to her door. I looked back at Hannah and saw her drive back towards her apartment.

When I reached the door, I knocked a few times.

The door then opened. "Hey, Elizabeth! Come on in!" Martha said.

"Thanks. How are you?" I said.

"I'm good. How are you?"

"Sore but fine."

I took a few steps into the apartment. Then I heard the door close behind me. There was a sound of a lock latching. And a sound of another lock latching. I didn't bother looking back at the door because I was sure that Martha was trying to be extra protective after what happened to me. There's no telling if there will be another Rita in these apartments after all.

"Make yourself comfortable, Elizabeth," Martha said. "Have a seat."

Despite my sore back, I sat on the couch and tried to get comfortable enough. As I sat down, I saw Martha walk into her bedroom.

I stared at her pictures on the wall while waiting for her to return. Martha always collected pictures of her family, friends, and herself and hung them on the wall. I didn't see a picture of me anywhere, which was not too shocking, seeing that we considered ourselves no longer friends at one point and just became best friends again not too long ago. I believe that she took a picture she used to have of us off the wall after our argument and has never had the chance to put it back up yet.

While looking at more pictures, I heard footsteps coming out of the bedroom. I looked over and saw Brandon and Tom with Martha. Once they got in front of me, Brandon and Tom stared me down with an angry look. I didn't know how to feel about that. I figured they were probably mad at me for what I did to them before Martha and I argued, but I wasn't sure.

"You guys having dinner with me and Martha?" I finally asked.

"Shut up, you bitch!" Tom yelled and slapped me in the face. As Tom slapped me, I fell to my side on the couch because of how much force Tom put into it.

Brandon immediately grabbed my hands and put them behind my back. He then tied them together with duct tape.

"What are you guys doing?!" I yelled.

"I said shut up!" Tom said and slapped me again.

"Martha! What's happ-?!" Tom put his hand over my mouth so I would stop yelling. While he did that, Brandon put duct tape around my ankles, taping them together.

Tom and Brandon got me into a sitting position on the couch, and Brandon put some duct tape on my mouth so Tom could get his hand off. As I mumbled under the tape, I looked around to see where Martha was. At first, I thought they were about to tie her up next. But then I saw Martha standing before me, giving me a smirk and not showing any sign of concern.

"Damn, Tom. You know how to impress a lady," Martha said as she wrapped her arms around Tom and kissed his cheek. I was utterly stunned by what I heard and what I was seeing.

"Anything for you, my princess," Tom said, looking down into Martha's eyes.

I mumbled with the duct tape on my mouth, attempting to ask Martha what was happening.

"Get that duct tape off her mouth. I want to hear what she has to say," she said.

Tom tore off the duct tape. "What is going on here?" I asked.

"Here's the funny story, Elizabeth. After we heard on the news that Rita got arrested and you were in the hospital, still alive, we felt we had to take matters into our own hands," Martha said.

"What are you talking about?"

"Rita is Brandon's girlfriend and our best friend. Because you had her arrested, we wanted to get back at you for it."

Hearing what Martha was saying left me more stunned by the minute. I couldn't believe Martha was calling Rita her best friend.

"How did she become your best friend? I thought I was your best friend."

"After what you did to Tom and Brandon, we are no longer friends. And seeing that Brandon is dating Rita now, we will be hanging out more often, which makes us best friends," Martha said with an angry smile.

"Martha, you don't want to do this. This is not you."

Martha chuckled and returned to staring at Tom in his eyes, her arms on his shoulders. "Brandon put the duct tape back on her."

"Hannah will be looking for me if..." Brandon put the duct tape on my mouth before I could finish that sentence.

"She won't be looking for you, Elizabeth. We already texted her on your phone, saying you would be staying here instead of her place. We also said that I would take care of you until you fully healed," Martha said. "Now, be a good friend and just stay there while Tom and I go watch a movie in the bedroom."

"I do like movies," Tom said.

Martha and Tom started walking toward Martha's bedroom. On the way there, Martha giggled a couple of times as if Tom was touching her in certain areas.

Once the bedroom door closed, I looked back at Brandon, who stood before me. I stared at him, feeling fear throughout my body. I was scared of what Brandon was going to do to me.

"We're going to have some fun as well," Brandon said, giving me an angry-looking smirk.

Brandon took a seat next to me and kept looking at me. He put his hand on my thigh.

"A lot of fun," he said.

My eyes widened, unsure of what he would do next. As he slid his hand up my thigh toward my crotch, more fear hit me. It hit me so hard. I started screaming under the duct tape, and that's when he grabbed the top of my jeans and quickly undid the zipper and button. I screamed more and more under the duct tape as he started to pull down my jeans past my thighs and knees.

He then grabbed my pink underwear and started pulling them down quickly. Once they were down far enough, he grabbed my legs and took the duct tape off my ankles. He then grabbed one of my ankles and held it towards the couch leg, where he put duct tape on it as well as my ankle. Then he did the same thing with my other ankle on the opposite couch leg. My legs were very uncomfortable in that position, but I could not move.

Brandon then removed his pants and boxers and threw them aside. Before I knew it, he sat on me with his knees resting on the couch cushion. Once Brandon got in the proper position, I felt him go inside me with his penis. After he was in, he started jerking back and forth at a fast pace.

"This is what happens when you send my girl to jail, you dumb bitch," he said as he was starting to breathe heavily.

I was moaning under the duct tape. I've never had anyone do this to me before. I've never even seen a penis before.

After roughly a minute, Brandon got out of me and then took my ankles off of the couch legs and tied them back together with a new piece of duct tape. He then put me in a lying position on the couch. That's when Brandon pulled my underwear and pants back up. After he finished, he stared into my eyes and gave me an evil smile.

"To be continued, bitch," he said.

Brandon then went to Martha's bedroom and said a couple of things to her before he walked out of the apartment. As I lay on the couch, I stared at the ceiling. Feeling numb and shocked, I couldn't believe what Brandon just did. What made him want to do that to me? Did he do it because he is mad at me for getting Rita arrested? Did he do it because he has sexual needs? Why?

I cried myself to sleep, wondering why Martha was letting this happen to me and what would happen next.

I opened my eyes and looked around. Looking at the clock on the wall, it was a little past six in the morning. I saw Martha sitting in her chair not too far from the couch, watching me like a hawk. My hands and arms were so sore from lying on them.

"Good morning, Elizabeth. Today will be a fun day," Martha said, coming to the couch. "You know why that is?"

She pulled the duct tape off my mouth when she reached the couch. "Why is that?" I said, my voice a little shaky out of fear.

"Because today, you will do whatever I say. Let me get this duct tape off you really quick."

Martha took the duct tape off my wrists, and I stretched my arms and swung them back and forth, trying to get rid of the feeling of the pain. She then took the duct tape off my ankles, and I got myself into a sitting position. I wanted to jump up and run so badly, but as I saw Martha grab a spatula, I got a little more scared and frightened to move.

"Now, if you don't follow my directions. I'll have to hit you with this spatula. And I surely don't want to do that," Martha said, tapping the spatula against the palm of her hand.

"Martha, what happened to you? Why are you doing this?" I asked.

"Shut up. Don't say anything unless I tell you to. The only reason I took the duct tape off your mouth was because I know that you would take it off yourself now that your hands are free," Martha said, pointing the spatula towards my face.

I was shaking from head to toe while waiting for her first order of direction.

"Now, to start with, make me some breakfast! Make me some scrambled eggs."

I slowly got up, continuously shaking with fear, knowing Martha followed my every move. Just one wrong move, and she could hit me with the spatula.

I cracked a couple of eggs into a bowl and accidentally got a piece of an eggshell into the mix. I immediately grabbed it out of the bowl, which Martha noticed.

"How dare you!" Martha said as she slapped the spatula against my back. The pain in my back was very sharp. So sharp I wanted to cry.

"Sorry," I said.

Then Martha slapped me in the back again. "I said no talking!"

I stirred the eggs and got them cooking in the frying pan. As I was watching them cook and moving the eggs around the pan, all I could think of was if I was doing something wrong again and about to get slapped again. I felt sweat drip down my forehead from the pan's heat and the fear I was experiencing. I kept biting my lower lip on and off. Not being restrained to the couch was the only good thing to consider now.

Once the eggs were done cooking, at least in my opinion, I put them onto a plate and turned off the stove. I then grabbed a fork and handed the plate to Martha.

"That's a good girl. Now, make some more eggs for Tom and Brandon," Martha said.

I rolled my eyes, feeling annoyed outside of fear, and cracked more eggs into a bowl. As I was stirring, I started to feel sad. I asked myself, 'Why did Martha turn out like this? Why is this stuff happening to me?' Thanks to the heat of the stove and the fear and sadness, I kept on feeling more sweat forming around my forehead.

Once I finished cooking those eggs, I again put them on a plate. I put them on the counter and then look at Martha, seeing what she has in store for me next.

"Very good. Now, sit on the couch," Martha said as she pointed the spatula toward the couch.

I returned to the couch, and Martha sat in her chair, eating her eggs while still holding the spatula and watching me like a hawk.

I was afraid to speak to her, but I had to ask, "Can I have breakfast?"

Martha stopped chewing and gave me an angry stare for a few seconds. She then set the plate down and came at me with the spatula. Only this time, she hit me in the side of my arm three times while I was attempting to block myself from her.

"I told you not to speak. And no. You don't deserve any food."

Tears formed in my eyes from the pain of the spatula. I attempted not to let them drip down my face in case Martha would hit me again upon seeing the tears, but that was a failure. All I could do at that point was try not to make any sound of crying and stay still while Martha ate her breakfast.

As she continued to eat her breakfast, I heard a door creak open from the back of the apartment. Then I heard footsteps.

"Morning, sweetheart!" Tom said, grabbing his plate of eggs. "Brandon just texted me saying he is on his way here."

"Morning, darling. I had Elizabeth make breakfast for us."

"Aw, you're sweet."

Tom came to the living room and leaned down to kiss Martha. He then sat down right next to me on the couch. As Tom sat on the couch, I jumped slightly at the thought he was sitting right next to me. Not knowing if he was going to do anything to me or not had me shaking in fear.

"You ready for work today?" Tom asked while continuing to eat his eggs.

"I'm never ready for work. I'm only ready to make the money," Martha said as she continued eating.

Seeing the two eat their breakfast made me more and more hungry by the second.

A few minutes later, there was a knock on the door. Just hearing the knock startled me. Although I had a gut feeling I knew who it was, anything would startle me at this point.

Martha went to open the door, and as I had expected, it was Brandon.

"Morning all," Brandon said as he walked in.

"Morning, Brandon. Breakfast is on the kitchen counter for you. I had Elizabeth make it for us," Martha said with a smile.

"Ooh. If this breakfast is any good, I must reward her."

My eyes widened at the thought of that. Something told me by 'reward,' he meant rape me once again. If not that, it's probably something worse.

Brandon went to the kitchen, grabbed his plate, and returned to the couch. Once he got to the couch, he sat on my other side. As he sat down, I started getting more and more shaky to where I was breathing slightly heavy but not so noticeably heavy.

Brandon, Tom, and Martha continued talking while eating their breakfast. At one point, Martha started talking about my past to them.

"You know, back in high school, Rita would always call Elizabeth 'lazybeth'." Martha said.

Brandon and Tom laughed along with Martha. I was shocked Martha would bring that up.

"Why was that?" Brandon laughed.

"I can't remember exactly. I think it was because Elizabeth was a loner and didn't get into activities."

I wanted to respond badly, but I knew I couldn't unless I wanted to get hit with the spatula again. All I could do was make an annoyed yet angry face and not say anything. Hearing that nickname brought back some harsh memories of high school.

"That's hilarious. This is why I love Rita. She is so creative and smart," Brandon said.

"For sure," Martha said.

After taking their last bites of breakfast, Martha grabbed all the plates and put them into the sink. When she returned and grabbed her spatula, she directed me to wash those dishes. Once again, she followed me with the spatula, watching my every move. Once I got to the sink, I turned on the water to soak the dishes. I grabbed the sponge and started to put soap on it.

Out of nowhere, Martha slaps me on the back with the spatula. "That's too much soap!"

I started scrubbing the dishes as I started panicking. I kept thinking to myself, 'When am I going to get slapped again?'

After cleaning the dishes, Martha directs me to sit back down.

"Before we get ready for work, I think Tom and I need a quickie," Martha said.

"I couldn't agree more," Tom said.

Martha starts to take off her pajama shirt and show off her boobs to Tom. Tom then grabs her boobs and starts cuddling her as she gets down on the floor with him. They were then kissing each other and caressing each other.

I kept trying to look away, not wanting to see them go crazy over each other the way they were, but that was nearly impossible.

Brandon stared at me as Tom removed Martha's pajama shorts. I immediately knew what he was thinking.

"You know what this means?" Brandon said.

I didn't respond to him, already knowing what he was about to say. All I did was show off fear in my face.

As Tom and Martha were starting to have intercourse with each other, Brandon grabbed the duct tape and put a piece over my mouth. He then grabbed my hand and jerked me onto the floor.

"Let's go bitch," Brandon said.

I mumbled under the duct tape, trying to say, 'Please don't,' but he didn't know what I was saying and likely didn't care.

As Brandon had me lay down on the floor, he sat over my legs to prevent me from kicking while he undid my jeans. He then pulled down my pants and underwear. Then he got his pants and boxers down and then positioned himself to get into me.

As he got inside me, all I could hear was Martha and Tom making sounds like animals.

Brandon started moving faster by the second. I began to mumble under the duct tape as if I was attempting to scream for help.

Once Brandon was done and got out of me, I felt a tear run down my cheek as I saw Martha and Tom just finishing up. Again, why is Martha letting this happen to me?

"That was sure a good quickie," Brandon said.

"Indeed, it was," Tom said.

"Tom, you are amazing!" Martha said.

"Not as amazing as you are, sweetheart."

Martha and Tom kissed one last time, and then Martha got up and headed to the bathroom.

"Brandon, we better tie her back up for when we go to work," Tom said.

"I'm on it," Brandon said.

Brandon grabbed me by the ankles and grabbed the duct tape. He then wrapped my ankles in the duct tape. Once he finished with that, Tom helped him by putting my hands behind my back while Brandon wrapped the duct tape around my wrists. They then lifted me and put me on the couch.

Tears continued to stream down my face while I sat on the couch. Brandon and Tom went to prepare themselves for work while I stared at the door, hoping for some miracle. The best miracle I could imagine was Hannah coming to my rescue like before. Or better yet, Lucky saving me once again. But because Martha mentioned how she texted Hannah from my phone last night, I had no hope.

There was still pain in my back, not only from the wounds that were still in the process of healing but also because of how Martha slapped my back with the spatula. With all the other pain going on emotionally and physically, it was like I didn't even notice the pain from my wounds at all. Even though, at certain times and movements, I would feel the pain, the pain of what's been going on pretty much felt worse than the back pain from the wounds.

Martha walked out of the bathroom wearing a simple T-shirt with her company logo and jeans. As Martha checked to ensure she had everything she needed, Tom walked out of Martha's bedroom, dressed for work, and Brandon followed right behind him.

"We will see you when we get back, Elizabeth," Martha said.

As Martha walked by me, she slapped me in the face. Being right behind her, Tom slapped me as he walked by. Finally, Brandon walked by and also slapped me in the face. All three looked back at me as they headed out the door. They gave me an evil smile as if they enjoyed seeing me in pain. A couple of seconds later, they closed the door behind them, and I was sitting on the couch alone, restrained by duct tape and unable to call for help, thanks to the duct tape on my mouth.

CHAPTER 15

After quite some time, I checked the clock to ensure Martha was at work and not likely to be coming back. I made attempts at spreading my wrists apart to where the duct tape would break. The first few times were unsuccessful. After I took a break due to my wrists hurting, I tried again. And again. And again.

After a few more attempts, I got this intense feeling of strength inside of me, and it made me want to pull my wrists apart harder and harder. By doing that, I finally broke the duct tape apart.

I immediately took the duct tape off my mouth and my ankles right after.

Once I was free from the duct tape restraints, I first thought of food. I was famished. I looked in Martha's cabinet for something quick and straightforward. I found a box of granola bars. I grabbed one and immediately ate it as fast as I could. While doing that, I saw my cell phone sitting on the counter.

After grabbing it, I walked to the door and opened it. I checked the screen door window to ensure Martha, Brandon, or Tom weren't in sight. I then opened the screen door and continued looking back and forth to make sure it was clear for me to escape. I stepped out, closed the door behind me, and looked around again. Seeing it was clear everywhere I looked, I ran towards Hannah's apartment building. At times, I felt some pain in my back. But no matter the pain, I kept running to escape.

Hannah's apartment seemed so far away from Martha's, but I eventually made it.

I opened the screen door. Hoping for a miracle, I turned the doorknob on the main door, and it was unlocked. I quickly opened the door and went inside Hannah's place, closing the door behind me and locking it.

Looking around Hannah's apartment while catching my breath, I didn't see Hannah anywhere. I didn't even see Lucky anywhere.

"Hannah?" I said loud enough that my voice could be heard in the other rooms.

There was no response at all.

"Lucky?" I said loud enough.

Still no response, and I didn't hear or see Lucky coming out from anywhere.

I grew a little worried at first, but then I remembered that Lucky probably needed to go outside for a walk or to the bathroom.

After I caught my breath, I walked through the apartment to see if Hannah and Lucky were anywhere.

I checked the bathroom, the bedroom, and the kitchen, but there was no sight of them.

After I had not seen them anywhere, I sat on the couch with my elbows on my knees, waiting for them to come home.

As I continued waiting, my phone started to ring. Hoping it was Hannah, I answered without looking at the caller ID.

"Hello?" I answered.

"Hey Elizabeth, come out to play," a woman's voice said.

"Who is this?"

"Take a guess."

I looked at the caller ID on my phone and didn't recognize the number at all. I knew it wasn't Martha because I would have recognized her voice easily. Since I didn't recognize the number, my next best guess was Rita sitting in county jail. "Rita?"

"No, silly. It's Maria. Are you looking for someone?"

"Maybe. Why do you ask?"

"Because I have your friend Hannah here with me and your husky, who doesn't know how to shut up."

I could hear Lucky barking in the background. "What are you doing with them?!"

"Oh, we're just taking a nice trip to the forest just outside of town."

"What forest outside of town?"

"The one that is near the Capitol. Are you that stupid?"

"Tell me you won't hurt them," I started feeling slightly shaky with fear.

"Just meet us there, and they won't get hurt. Call this number back once you see the capitol building, and I'll lead you to where I'm at."

Maria then hung up the phone, and not knowing what to think, I got up and went to look for my keys. While looking, I noticed that Hannah had a Springfield Armory XD-M pocket pistol on her counter. Never in my life have I used a gun, and I've never seen anyone shoot them except for television shows.

I felt very hesitant, being that I never shot a gun; I felt like I had no choice but to grab it and hide it in the waistline between my jeans and belly. It was for the safety of Hannah and Lucky, I kept reminding myself. I also told myself there was no telling what Maria had up her sleeve this time.

Eventually, I found my keys on the side table near Hannah's couch and then left to go towards the state capitol.

CHAPTER 16

Driving down the highway, I saw nothing but the road. There was a decent amount of traffic on the highway, but I could only stare at the road I followed. I focused on nothing but thinking about what Maria could be up to now.

My mind was racing. Was Maria going to kill Hannah or Lucky as revenge for Matt getting killed, even though it wasn't my fault? I was seriously hoping she wasn't hurting them in any way possible.

I kept imagining the worst while approaching the state capitol exit.

As I approached a stop sign, I noticed a sign that said 'state park' with an arrow pointing to the right. I was unsure if Maria meant that area or another area. I only knew that she was in some area near the state capitol.

With that, I made a right turn and crossed my fingers that this was the right direction.

I've never been to the state capitol before. It was fascinating seeing the Capitol building in person instead of on television.

After following the road for some time, I noticed some interesting buildings. Some were tall and appeared primarily to be windows, and some were connected in odd shapes (like one almost shaped like the letter H). I also noticed some attractions that would be interesting to see. Too bad I don't have the money or time for them. That shows that I need to travel more now that I am on my own, especially since this area is not too far from Bay City.

Seeing those buildings made me realize I haven't been able to enjoy life so much. Living with my mom made that near impossible. Although Martha and I had fun together, we never had fun by checking out different places.

Once I started working at the diner, I didn't want to spend a penny because of how little I made, which is another reason I didn't get to do fun things and live my life a little bit. It made me sad, especially knowing that I could be facing the chance of losing my life yet again.

After hearing a prolonged, ongoing horn honking, I snapped out of thinking about how sad that was. I looked ahead and saw a car right in front of me heading towards me. I immediately turned my steering wheel to the right. I heard my tires screeching as I attempted to straighten out my car. However, my car hit a traffic light pole in the middle of the roadway on a median.

The airbag came out in front of me. I kept trying to get it out of my way and looked out the windshield. The traffic pole I hit was slightly bent to the side. I could see the front of my car had some damage on the top of the hood, but I was scared to look at the rest of the front edge and see how hard I hit the pole.

I opened the car door and got out. Realizing I wasn't in any more pain than I already was, I walked up to the front of the vehicle. The front end got severely dented, and the car's hood bent to a triangular shape. I saw pieces of the front end in different places around the area.

Putting my hands on my mouth in shock, I couldn't believe what had happened to my car. This car was my only way of transportation. It was one of the most essential things in my life. And the most expensive thing I had ever bought.

Looking around, I saw people driving by while staring at my car. The only thing I could think of at that moment was how I still needed to save Hannah and Lucky.

Thinking about that, I checked my pocket to ensure my phone was there. I also checked the part of my pants to make sure the gun was still there. Thankfully, they both were.

With that, I started running towards the direction I was going. As weak feeling as I was, just thinking of saving Hannah and Lucky made me want to go faster.

I approached a sign that said, 'Welcome to Carvmon Park.' After all the running I had done, I hoped this was the park Maria was talking about. As Maria had said, it wasn't too far from the Capitol.

There were so many trees surrounding the area. There was also cement trail with a yellow line in the middle divided the area into lanes for walkers and bikers in each direction.

I got my phone out of my pocket and called the number Maria had called me from, hoping she would answer so I could get some direction.

"Hello," Maria said once she picked up the phone.

"Maria, I'm at Carvmon Park. Is this the park you are at?"

"Yes."

"Where are you in the park?"

"It's easy. Just follow the trail until you reach the cliff."

"Cliff? Please tell me you won't throw Hannah and Lucky off the cliff."

"I guess you will have to find out for yourself."

Maria hung up, and at that point, I was so scared for the two that I knew I had to hurry.

I followed the trail as she said. Only this time, I was speed walking since I was starting to get weak and didn't have enough energy to run anymore. I was hoping that the cliff was pretty close.

Speed walking on the trail for about fifteen minutes, I saw nothing but trees. I saw the occasional jogger or bicyclist going in the opposite direction as me. Whenever I saw someone pass by me in the opposite direction, I wondered if they happened to see Maria with Hannah and Lucky. If so, why were they looking so calm and focused on where they were going?

My feet were slowly starting to hurt with every step I took. Whenever I felt pain in my feet or legs, I hoped I was closer to the cliff.

As I slowed down, I noticed a yellow sign that said, 'Caution: Cliff ahead'. Hoping this was the cliff I had been looking for, I picked up speed again.

Walking closer to the edge, I noticed a figure sitting against a tree. I also saw what appeared to be another figure standing right next to it. It was hard to tell at first if it was Maria and Hannah, but something told me that it was them, and that made me keep going despite the pain and weakness.

"Oh, look who finally made it," I heard the figure say as I got closer.

I walked towards the voice, and as I predicted, I saw Maria. I also saw Hannah tied to the tree she was sitting at with a rope around her waist. That rope also had her arms tied to her side so she couldn't move them. Her mouth was full of some cloth to make it so she couldn't speak.

I also saw Lucky tied to a tree. The rope was tied over his body and around his legs to where he could not move. His mouth, however, was not tied up. He remained quiet, likely because of fear.

"Hannah!" I said in shock after seeing what Maria did to her.

"Don't worry, Elizabeth. Hannah here is fine. I would be worried about you," Maria said, walking past Hannah and towards me.

"Why do you say that?"

"You see if Matt had not been with you that one night, he would not have died. But thanks to you, he is dead."

"And how is that my fault? The killer told me she meant to stab me and not him."

"Like I said, if he weren't with you that night, he would have not been killed. Me and him would have probably been enjoying a night together."

"How does that make me want to worry about myself?"

"Well, first, I need to show you what losing a friend is like—losing a close friend. Just like what you did to me with Matt. After you see what happens when you lose a friend, then we will figure out what to do with you as punishment forgetting Matt killed."

"The killer is behind bars now. It's NOT MY FAULT!" I was getting more irritated the more she said it was my fault Matt died.

"Doesn't matter! If he weren't there with you, he wouldn't have died!" Maria started walking towards the edge of the cliff. "Now let me show you something."

I started following her, although part of me felt I shouldn't because she might push me off the cliff's edge. We stood about ten steps away from the edge of the cliff.

"Take a good look down there, Elizabeth," Maria said, pointing downwards at the cliffs edge. "You see all those rocks? It'll be like you were skydiving without a parachute once I push you off that cliff. Just imagine what will happen when your head hits those rocks."

I gulped at the thought of that. I didn't want to imagine what would happen once I was pushed off the cliff. The cliff was at least one-hundred feet high. The ground below the cliff was covered entirely with large rocks. Not a sight of water or grass or trees.

I looked back at Maria, and she gave me an evil smile. "Look on the bright side; I'll be throwing your stupid friend and stupid dog off this first so you can see what will happen to you. Won't that be fun to watch?"

I slightly shook my head with a look of fear on my face.

"Well, I know I will have fun watching this."

"Maria," I said as my voice got shaky. "I know you're upset about Matt's death. I am, too. I don't think this is the way to settle this."

"Oh, this is the way to settle this. After all, you need to see what losing a friend is like. A very close friend."

"It's not my fault he got killed."

"Shut up! It's your fault, and you know it!" Maria walked up to me; her face pretty close to mine. She looked at me square in the eye with an angry look, "As I said earlier, nothing would have happened to him if he weren't with you that night."

"But..."

"Shut up! I was mad enough when he chose you over me as a girlfriend. But once I heard he died, I knew you were to blame."

Maria took a step backward.

"Is that why you attempted to run me over with your car at the police station?"

"You know it. And that's why you saw me say you were next. Because of you. Matt is dead, and I knew I had to do something in honor of his death. And what better way to honor his death than to kill the girl who had him killed."

"Then let my friends go. You want to kill me for the most part. Why capture my friends and attempt to kill them?"

Maria rolled her eyes, "Do you ever listen? You need to see what losing a close friend is like."

Maria started walking around me in circles, ensuring I was not making any sudden moves. With one hand on her hip, she kept talking while I stood there and listened because I felt like if I made a sudden move, I would get pushed off the cliff.

"When I saw Matt at the restaurant where I was working, I knew it was fate, saying it was time for us to get back together. However, when I saw you, I knew I had to do something to get him away from you. That's why I stalked you and Matt on your little dates. I was waiting for the perfect reason to tell Matt you didn't deserve him. While doing so, I was also trying to figure out how to win his heart back."

After she said that, I smirked and rolled my eyes, thinking, 'I knew it!'

"That one morning, I went into your diner," she continued, "I thought it was the perfect time to chat with him and win him back. But he didn't see how much I loved him for some reason. I doubt it was because of my recent arrest; he wouldn't know about it because he was out of town for college."

I smirked again, thinking sarcastically, 'shocker.'

Maria suddenly stopped in front of me. "Once he told me we were just friends, I was devastated, but I still felt the need to find something wrong with you. And I think I finally found it. But it's too late to show Matt."

"What did you find?"

"I found that you are nothing but bad luck. After seeing the news about the person who kidnapped you, I knew I had to dig deeper somehow. After all, how is it that Matt dies, and you end up getting kidnapped soon after? The only way I could think of at first was that you are a narcissist trying to get attention for yourself. Then I found a newspaper with your name on it about your house getting burnt down by your mother.

"Seeing the fire and the kidnapping stories made me realize you are bad luck. Of course, Matt getting killed while with you proves it, too. If Matt were alive today, he would run away from you and return to me. That's why, when you were in the hospital after the kidnapping, I was able to hack the system and pose as a nurse, saying that it was time for you to get discharged. Once that happened, I started coming up with my plan for revenge."

"If you loved him so much, why did you cheat on him?"

"I didn't cheat on him! We took a break when he was out of state for college, and I happened to be with another guy. At first, I felt I wouldn't be able to see Matt again, which is why I met a guy at a club. After dancing with him, I decided to give him a chance. So, we started dating.

"Before I knew it, he broke it off with me. But I wasn't ready to get rid of him, so I tried to do what I could to get back with him. After that failed, I felt the need to give him revenge. After all, you'll be sorry when you hurt this girl, as I always say. Which is why you will be sorry, Elizabeth. You seriously hurt me by having Matt killed, and now it's time I get my revenge," Maria stepped close to get close to my face. "Got anything to say about that?"

"Yes. Is that a spider on your shoe?"

Maria looked towards her feet in fear. "What? Where?!"

I grabbed Maria by the upper arms and pushed her down to the ground. I then went down to her after she was on the ground. She kept trying to push me off of her and wanted to hurt me somehow to get off of her.

As I started to try to hold her down with my body, I pulled the gun out of my pants. Then Maria rolled me over and pinned me down while taking the gun from my hand.

"Ha!" Maria said, pointing the gun at me. "Looks like I have a better way of making this fun happen!"

I lay on the ground in silence as I stared at the gun. I was feeling very disappointed in myself for not being able to get rid of Maria once and for all.

"Time to say goodnight, Elizabeth Monter!"

As I continued to stare at the gun barrel that was pointing right at me, I suddenly saw Maria drop the gun as she screamed. Maria stumbled backward and suddenly disappeared. I heard an echo of her scream as the sound went farther and farther away.

After staring at the sky for some time, I look towards the cliff and saw Lucky was there, free from the tree.

Overjoyed, I immediately got myself off the ground and ran towards Lucky to hug him.

"Lucky! You're free! And you saved me once again," I couldn't stop hugging him.

After petting Lucky and briefly hugging him, I remembered Hannah still needed to be free from the tree.

I ran towards her and got the cloth out of her mouth.

"Elizabeth," she said after I got the cloth out of her mouth.

"Hannah, I'm glad you're okay."

I started untying the rope where Maria knotted it. It wasn't the easiest knot to untie, but I eventually got it.

"Me too. You should've seen what Lucky did to save you."

I smiled at Lucky as he approached Hannah and me. I started to pet him. "What did he do?"

"Once Maria was pointing the gun at you, he started biting on the rope he was tied up with to break it off. At first, I thought that was impossible, but he somehow managed to break it. Once he was free from that, he ran towards Maria and bit her leg so hard that she stumbled backward and fell off the cliff. As she fell. Lucky started smiling with his tongue hanging out. I'm guessing he was happy that you were safe."

"I don't know if I would have survived without Lucky."

"I'm not sure how I would've survived. I don't know how to thank you enough for all that you did to save me," A tear started to form in Hannah's eye as she continued talking. "To come to the State Capitol and risk your life for me and Lucky. That's the bravest thing anyone has ever done for me."

"Hannah," I put my hand on her shoulder, "You saved me that one day Rita was after me. I don't know how to thank you for that except for saving you somehow."

"I guess we are even on that," Hannah smiled and chuckled.

I chuckled and smiled along with her.

"Just one more thing," I said. "My car crashed. How are we going to get home?"

"Well, we will have to call the police about Maria falling off the cliff at some point," Hannah said. "Maybe they will take us home."

I nodded and got my phone out of my pocket to call the police.

CHAPTER 17

Epilogue

Two Months Later

" **A**nd how do you feel about that, Elizabeth?" said the psychologist I was having a session with.

I looked down and rubbed my belly. My slowly but surely growing belly. I found out not too long ago I got pregnant by Brandon. I was not ready to have a child, but at the same time, I saw it as a reason for me to live and be happy. I've always dreamed of having a mini-me, but not like this. Not this soon in my life.

"I'm excited about having a child, but I'm sad the child won't have a father," I said. "I'm also scared because I know I'm not in the best financial state."

After all the events that took place, I was in the hospital for some time. With that, I lost my job. I tried to explain to Barbara what had happened, and she seemed to understand, but sadly, she couldn't let me continue working there. For now, I've been receiving unemployment and living with Hannah. Although I've been looking for a job, my psychologist, Amber, suggested I take a break to gather my emotions from the events.

Lucky has been my emotional support through the challenging emotional times I've been going through, along with seeing the psychologist. Whenever I'm feeling down, Lucky can sense it and come to cuddle with me.

Hannah has also been accommodating regarding my emotional problems. She has also helped take care of Lucky and me when necessary. I don't know how I could've survived without her.

I called the police after Maria fell to her death; I told them about the events that involved Martha, Tom, and Brandon. Not long after reporting them, they got arrested in the parking lot of their work.

During the investigation, it was found that after Maria hacked the hospital computer and discharged me, Martha saw me walking into Hannah's apartment. Martha then got ahold of Hannah's number and posed as one of her coworkers, saying she needed to get to the dealership as soon as possible. Martha did that to get the chance to fake apologize to me for what she did and get a head start on making me fall into her trap.

Martha, Tom, and Brandon currently sit in Bay City jail, charged with unlawful restraints, battery, and kidnapping. Of course, Brandon also got charged with rape.

I never told Brandon myself that I got pregnant from him raping me. However, the police brought it up to him during questioning, so he is indeed aware that I'm pregnant with his child.

Rita continues to remain in jail while awaiting trial for kidnapping and attempted murder.

I'm not looking forward to facing all four of them in future trials. The only thing I will look forward to involving them is hearing them having to rot in prison for a reasonable amount of time.

I walked into Hannah's apartment, and like any time I stepped inside, Lucky came running towards me and sometimes jumped on me, wanting me to pet him. He always puts a smile on my face.

"Hey, how did the session go?" Hannah asked.

"It went alright. I mainly talked about the baby. As I keep saying, I'm excited but scared," I said.

"Everything will work out, I'm sure."

"Yeah, I'm sure. I just have to be patient and try my best to get through this tough time."

"Did you hear that the police released information on Maria?"

"No, what did they say?"

"I recorded it once I saw it. I'll show you."

Hannah pressed a few buttons on her TV remote and went to a recording she had from the news channel today while I got myself comfy on the couch. Once she hit play, it showed Maria's mugshot from her arrest months earlier and started talking about her.

"Maria Frichmen was found dead two months ago in Carv-mon Park," the news anchor said. "The cause of death was the impact from falling off a one-hundred-and-fifty-foot cliff. Here's Mark Prickle with the story."

"Thank you, Randy. I'm here at the Carvmon Park cliff where the incident occurred," Mark said. "Maria Frichmen was at this location with two other people and a dog that she planned on killing. Because of the dog breaking the rope Maria tied him up with, the dog was able to bite Maria in the leg, which caused her to stumble backwards to the edge of this cliff, where she fell to her death.

"Police investigated the dog further and discovered he was protecting his owner. His owner was on the ground at gun-point, and once the dog saw that, he sprang into action to save her.

"Maria had kidnapped the dog and a friend of the dog owner and then made the owner meet her out here so Maria could kill them all.

"Investigators found that Maria previously got arrested for attempted murder after stabbing an ex-boyfriend's girlfriend. When she got arrested, she was diagnosed with narcissistic personality disorder. It was found that Maria had an excessive need for admiration and disregard for others' feelings. She has always wanted attention for herself from certain people, including boyfriends who broke it off with her. After a boyfriend broke up with her, she would take drastic measures to get the boyfriend back. That includes stalking, hacking accounts, and, in this case, killing the girlfriend.

"In the case at Carvmon Park, Maria was seeking revenge because an ex-boyfriend was stabbed to death while on a date with another woman. After hearing the news of that, Maria plotted to kill the victim's girlfriend. Maria claimed that if that ex-boyfriend hadn't been with her that night, he wouldn't have died.

"Maria kidnapped the dog and the victim's friend not only to lure the victim to her but also to show the victim what it was like to lose a friend by eventually planning to kill them as well. Thankfully, all victims survived. Back to you, Randy."

Hearing that Maria had narcissistic personality disorder was not surprising. The way she stalked me and Matt and kept blaming me for his death, I had that feeling she was something of a narcissist.

"Well, that doesn't surprise me," I said after Hannah stopped the recording.

"Really?" Hannah said.

"Yeah. Maria kept stalking me and my boyfriend, who was also her ex. She even attempted to get him back with her at one point. And as you probably heard on the cliff, she kept blaming me for his death. What I don't get is why was she thinking I was the narcissist and not admitting she was."

"She probably didn't want to come to terms with what she was, and she tried to make that a reason you shouldn't have been with her ex."

"That would make sense."

"Look on the bright side; you don't have to worry about her anymore."

"I know. I still wish Matt was here, though."

Lucky sensed sadness hitting me as I thought of Matt and immediately licked my face and rubbed his head against me.

"Oh, Lucky, what would I do with you?" I said as I started petting his head.

"Probably suffer," Hannah said.

"I know I would have suffered without you, Hannah," I laughed.

"Is it about time to take Lucky on a walk?"

"Yeah. Let's go for a walk, Lucky."

Lucky enjoys walking to a nearby park with a fenced-in area where dogs can play off their leashes with other dogs. So, when I take him on walks, I try to go to that park so he can have fun. Sometimes, I spoil him too much.

Lucky appeared to be having a wonderful time at the dog park. He and the other dogs sometimes played with a ball and chased each other.

"Looks like they're having fun. Don't you think?" a woman sitting next to me said. I looked at the woman while she talked and wondered exactly why she was talking to me.

I noticed her bleach-blonde straight hair and a ton of makeup on her face. Her lips appeared to have somewhat bright red lip liner with pink lipstick. She also had a lot of orange eye shadow and a ton of black eyeliner. Aside from the makeup, she wore a necklace with a silver flower and medium-sized hoop earrings. She was wearing a dark purple V-neck T-shirt and light blue jeans.

After my recent experiences, I had trust issues when meeting new people. I've always been afraid that whoever I meet will somehow try to kill me or do something terrible to me. At the same time, I'm not one to be rude and completely ignore someone unless they show obvious signs of wanting to do something terrible.

"Sure does," I said. "Which dog is yours?"

"The Dalmatian with the purple collar around her neck. Which one is yours?"

"The Siberian husky with the blue-collar."

"He looks so cute! What's his name?"

"Lucky. And your dog?"

"Her name is Diamond. It feels just like yesterday I picked her up from the pet store."

"Cute name. Diamond seems to be having fun with Lucky."

"Yeah. Diamond gets along with almost every dog she meets. I couldn't have asked for a better dog. I'm Katie Meyer, by the way. What's your name?"

Katie put out her hand and asked for a handshake.

"Elizabeth Monter. Nice to meet you," I shook Katie's hand.

"Nice to meet you as well. We should exchange numbers and hang out sometime."

Although I usually wait and exchange numbers after I hang out with people at least a couple of times, I figured that I would give her a shot and give her my number, especially since Lucky seems to be having fun with Diamond. Although I don't know if I should trust her, Katie seemed nice, and I'm sure Lucky will want to meet up with Diamond again at some point.

"Thanks, Elizabeth. I will talk to you later. Unfortunately, Diamond and I have to go," Katie said after we exchanged numbers.

"Okay. Have a good day," I said.

After Katie and Diamond left the park, I let Lucky play for a little longer. As I sat down and watched Lucky play some more, the image of Katie ran through my head. Something seemed off about her, but I couldn't pinpoint it.

The shape of her face reminded me of someone. Someone I had problems with before. But who?

After thinking about it for some time, I got Lucky to come over to me and put his leash back on so we could head back to the apartment.

While walking back towards the apartment, I tried to figure out why Katie looked so familiar, but I still couldn't wrap my mind around it. I was unsure if I was overthinking about her possibly being a bad person because of my past experiences or if my gut was telling me not to trust her at all.

When Lucky and I entered the door, I saw someone sitting on the couch. When the person turned to look at me, my heart started racing. It was Katie. How did she find out where I lived?

"Hey, Elizabeth," Katie said.

"Hey, Katie. How did you know where I lived?" I said as I got Lucky's leash unhooked.

"I didn't. I was moving into the apartment next door, and Hannah told me to stop by and take a break. So here I am."

"Next door?" I was a bit shocked.

I wondered if that was just a coincidence or something was happening.

"I just moved to Bay City, and this apartment complex seemed like the perfect place to stay. Between unpacking, I took Diamond for a walk to view the walking path and found the park where you and I met."

Feeling more hesitant about being friends with her, I pretended to sound happy, saying, "Welcome to Bay City. We're glad to have you as our neighbor."

"Thank you. I can already tell all three of us will be best friends."

I didn't know how to feel about that exactly.

As I sat down next to Katie on the couch, Hannah went back to talking with Katie. The two were talking to each other so much that I had no chance of getting a word in. They exchanged numbers at one point and mentioned how we need to have a weekly hangout, like at a coffee shop or something.

"We could go to the mall together or a coffee shop every week," Hannah said.

"That would be great. We will make it a girls' day out. Or, in some cases, a girls' night out if you guys want to go to the club with me," Katie said.

I would definitely enjoy a girls' night out, but only if it was with Hannah because, again. I'm having doubts about Katie, and I still can't pinpoint why that is.

"What do you think of that, Elizabeth?" Hannah said, looking towards me.

At that moment, I felt like I had no say in it. I wanted to tell Hannah how I felt about it, but I had to wait until Katie returned to her apartment. With that, I didn't want to ultimately hurt Katie's feelings, at least not yet.

"Sounds great," I said in a monotone.

"Awesome! I better get back to unpacking. I will talk to you later, besties!"

Katie left, and Hannah looked at me.

"You didn't seem excited about that, Elizabeth," Hannah said.

"Something about her doesn't feel right," I said.

"What do you mean? She seems pretty nice."

"She does, but for some reason, when I see her face minus the makeup, I feel like I recognize that person."

"Like who? Rita or Martha?"

"No. Not them. Someone who I've dealt with before, but I can't put my finger on it."

"I'm sure it's nothing. You're probably just still dealing with those past experiences to where you see an enemy in everyone but me."

"Maybe. I don't know. This might drive me up the wall for a while. So, if I act strange around Katie, you know why. Just don't tell her anything, please."

"Of course, I won't."

I lay back on the couch while continuously thinking about who it could be. It's not Rita, certainly not Martha, and nowhere near my mom. Who would it be? I hope that at one of our hangouts, Katie will not have so much makeup on so I can determine whether my gut is right or wrong. Once I see her actual face, I will know for sure if I should always trust my gut when it comes to people or if I should not always trust my gut.

About the Author

Brittany P. Joseph has been writing since she was a little girl. She has an Associates and Bachelors degree in Criminal Justice. She realized she has a passion for writing songs and stories and combined with writing talents with her education and came up with *The Worst of Luck*. She plans on writing more books in the future. Aside from writing, she also enjoys crafting and nature walks.

www.ingramcontent.com/pod-product-compliance
Lightning Source LLC
Chambersburg PA
CBHW070013140726
47908CB00020B/1280